War at the Diamond O

Hunting the outlaw Buck Dunne for killing his brother, Hilt rode into the Diamond O as ambushers tried to kill Chuck and Sue Ormond. Because a woman was being shot at, Hilt took a hand and was plunged instantly into a battle against heavy odds. Gunsmoke blossomed across the range, as he took on all-comers in his self-imposed chore to save the Ormonds.

As the shooting spread it seemed that everyone in the county was against him. Hilt clenched his teeth and continued to use his deadly gun. But would he survive the warfare and be able to hunt down the outlaw who had killed his brother?

War at the
Diamond O

CORBA SUNMAN

A Black Horse Western

ROBERT HALE · LONDON

© Corba Sunman 2003
First published in Great Britain 2003

ISBN 0 7090 7303 8

Robert Hale Limited
Clerkenwell House
Clerkenwell Green
London EC1R 0HT

Typeset by
Derek Doyle & Associates, Liverpool.
Printed and bound in Great Britain by
Antony Rowe Limited, Wiltshire

ONE

Hilt reached the crest of a long slope on the Texas side of the Mexican border and reined in to let the buckskin have a breather while he surveyed the vista that had unfolded before him. A line of low hills rose in the background, grey and oppressive, backed by craggy mountains that were blued by distance. His narrowed brown eyes, shadowed by his down-pulled hatbrim, flicked across the foreground of the featureless range as he looked for movement. Checking the middle distance, he saw the clustered buildings of a cattle ranch shimmering in the heat of high noon and spotted dust drifting from a corral where a wrangler was breaking in a mustang. He prepared to move on, hoping to get a riding job at the ranch, although he was reluctant to return to the yoke of raising cattle. But, he thought bitterly, anything would be better than his present way of life. He needed a break from man-hunting.

Through circumstance rather than preference, he had gained notoriety with his gun. The act of avenging the death of his younger brother six years before had saddled him with a reputation he could not live down, for it stuck to him despite his efforts to avoid it. The ensuing years, in which he had killed nine men, mainly in self-defence, saw his reputation grow by leaps and bounds. Raw kids and gun-slammers had accosted him with simulated quarrels, hoping to gain the dubious distinction of beating him to the draw, although all they had proved was that they were not in his class; had less talent with a gun.

He eased his tall, lean body in the saddle, scanning his surroundings, ever alert, for his vigilance was all that stood between him and death. Constantly on the move, seeking the third of the killers who had slain his brother, he had to make an effort to avoid the attentions of gun-crazy fools or the kin of those he had killed. But he had come to accept at last that there was no escape from the deadly turmoil dogging him.

He had learned that at least three men were looking for him – kin of some of those he had slain – and his mind and body were geared to the task of locating that elusive third killer, Buck Dunne, whom he wished to see through gunsmoke.

He twisted in the saddle to survey his dusty back trail, hardly aware of his instinctive alertness, which was now second nature and had saved his life on several occasions during his years of riding the lonely trails of the great South-West. He saw nothing to cause alarm but did not relax.

He had heard that Buck Dunne, having robbed a bank over in Bitter Creek, was now making for the Mexican border, and several lawmen were on the trail of the criminal. It had been the lure of the bounty on the heads of the three Dunne brothers that had been the downfall of Hilt's brother, Thad Hilton. The youngster had foolishly tried to collect the reward money offered for the Dunnes, and paid the grim price of failure.

Hilt caught a movement off to the far right and leaned forward in his saddle to peer intently at a fast-moving cloud of dust that had suddenly appeared over a rise and was boring along the narrow trail leading to the distant ranch.

Reaching into a saddle-bag, his fingers closed on a pair of field-glasses, and he raised them to his eyes, quickly bringing the banner of dust into focus. His teeth clicked together when he saw a buckboard being hauled by a pair of runaway horses. Two figures were on the high seat of the vehicle; one, a man, was slumped sideways and apparently unconscious, the other, a female, was hauling on the reins in a vain attempt to halt the runaways. The echoing sound of a shot reached his keen ears and he quickly switched his attention to the rear of the buckboard. Two riders were galloping into view over the rise, riding hard to overhaul the vehicle. Another shot echoed, and gunsmoke blossomed around the head and shoulders of one of the pursuers.

The man in the buckboard suddenly twisted around to face his back trail, making hard work of lifting a rifle from between his knees. He worked the mechanism of the weapon and fired, the flat crack of the shot sending echoes across the range. Hilt thrust the glasses back into his saddle-bag and shook the

7

reins. The buckskin started down the slope, quickly lifted into a gallop, and Hilt angled to intercept the wildly jolting vehicle. Bending low in the saddle, he urged the horse forward, riding with hands and heels, pushing for the buckskin's best speed.

He slid his Winchester out of the saddle scabbard and cocked it, not concerned about the rights and wrongs of the situation because there was a girl on the buckboard and the two pursuers were shooting at her. He dropped the knotted reins to the neck of the buckskin and lifted his rifle. Gunsmoke enveloped him when he fired and, although he did not expect to score a hit, he saw his target swerve violently and then look around hurriedly. Hilt fired again, this time aiming for the running horse.

The animal fell in a heap, its legs threshing. The rider flew through the air in an arc before hitting the ground and lying inert. The second rider reined in instantly. Hilt urged the buckskin to greater effort and quickly gained on the buckboard. He slid the Winchester back into its scabbard. The girl was still trying to stop the runaways. Hilt spurred his mount and swept past the rocking vehicle to snatch at the bridle of the nearest horse.

Using his considerable strength, Hilt hauled on the bridle while slowing his mount, and managed to gain control of the runaways. They slackened speed, and he spoke soothingly, easing them to a halt, when they stood with heads lowered and flanks heaving. He twisted in his saddle, looking for trouble, and tension seeped out of him when he saw that the remaining pursuer had dismounted beside his fallen pard and was in the act of heaving the inert man up across his saddle. Even as Hilt watched, the man mounted behind his pard and rode back the way they had come.

Hilt took notice of the departing horse, and was satisfied that he would know it again. He stepped down from his saddle and turned to look at the girl, who was hunched on the seat of the buckboard, her face ashen with shock. She was cradling the slumped body of her companion.

'Are you hurt?' Hilt demanded, reaching up to grasp her arm, for in her shock she did not appear to register his presence.

She started nervously, her eyes seemingly unfocused, and he noticed that they were startlingly blue and she was beautiful.

'I'm all right!' she gasped. 'But my father is hurt.'

Hilt walked around the buckboard and stepped up on the front wheel. The man was unconscious. There was blood on his coat. Hilt bared the man's chest to reveal a bullet wound some two inches under the left collar bone. A trickle of blood was oozing quickly from the exit wound. Easing the limp figure forward, Hilt examined the man's back to find an entry wound in the left clavicle. He nodded, his stiff features relaxing a little.

'I think he'll pull through,' he opined. 'Is that your place yonder?'

'Yes. The Diamond O. My father is the owner, Chuck Ormond. I'm Sue Ormond.'

'Pleased to know you.' As he spoke, Hilt untied his neckerchief, shook dust out of it, and then used it as a pad under the rancher's shirt, covering the exit wound. 'Hold that in place,' he instructed. He waited until her fingers were pressing against the pad then turned to pick up his reins. He tied the buckskin to the tailboard and then climbed up on the high seat, easing the man along it towards the girl and taking up the reins.

'We'd better get him to the ranch.' Hilt urged the team into motion, his voice harsh as he encouraged them. 'He'll need a doctor,' he added. 'Where's the nearest? Someone better make tracks for him, pronto.'

'Cedar Creek is the nearest town. Twelve miles to the south-east. I'll send in one of the hands soon as we get to the ranch.'

'Who were those men chasing you?' He glanced sideways at her, noting her degree of shock, but her chin was set firmly despite the daze showing in her eyes. She was young, probably in her early twenties, he surmised.

'That's what I mean to find out,' she responded. 'They came out of a draw and started shooting without warning. They looked like strangers.'

'Strangers don't start shooting for no reason at all, unless they reckoned to rob you.'

'I didn't wait to check their intention. Their first shot struck my father.' She studied him for a moment. 'You're a stranger.'

'I was on my way to your spread, hoping to get hired.'

'You're mighty handy with a rifle. I saw what you did back there. That was good shooting, and I hope you killed that snake you hit.' She moistened her lips and blinked rapidly as she tried to get her shock under control. 'We don't need extra cow hands at this time, but there's a job for you, if you want it.'

'Thanks. But I'm looking for a riding job and it sounds like you're wanting to hire my gun.'

'I'll take you on any terms. If Dad lives he'll be out of the saddle for weeks so I'll be doing the hiring and firing.' She subjected him to an intense scrutiny. 'But any man we hire these days will be expected to use his gun, if necessary.'

'Sounds like you're plumb full of trouble. I'll take a job with you.' Hilt spoke without hesitation. She had been shot at by apparent strangers and, although he did not believe in butting into the affairs of other people, he had been drawn into the situation. Having exchanged lead with the strangers, he wanted to know more about the business. 'A couple of riders are coming from the ranch,' he observed, alert to their surroundings.

'The rider on the grey is my brother Billy.' She shaded her eyes with an unsteady hand. 'The other is our ranch foreman, Art Weston.'

'I'll pull up here and get down.' He hauled on the reins. 'You'll manage now without me. I'll go back and check on those two strangers who ambushed you. I'll come back to the ranch after I've had a look around.'

She protested, but nodded as he jumped to the ground. He untied his buckskin and swung into the saddle. Turning the horse, he rode away, heading for the downed horse lying back along the trail. Behind him the sound of rapidly approaching hoofs hammered out the silence and he twisted in his saddle to watch the two men riding up to the buckboard. The younger of the two waved a hand to him, motioning for him to wait, and he reined in and sat the buckskin patiently, his face expressionless.

The older man reined in beside the buckboard and sprang out of his saddle. He was large, pushing middle age, raw-boned, slab-muscled, his heavy face showing age as he glanced in Hilt's direction. But he was intent upon the wounded rancher, and Hilt watched him carry out a swift examination, then pick up the reins of the team and whip the horses into motion, hurrying towards the distant ranch.

The younger man approached Hilt with a rush and hauled his grey to a slithering halt, raising dust. He resembled the girl, and looked to be in his late teens. His smooth, unlined face was pale with shock.

'I wanta thank you for helping out,' he gasped. 'Did you get a look at those two galoots?'

'Yeah. But I'm a stranger.' Hilt shook his head. 'I never saw them before.'

'But you'll know them again?' There was eagerness in the youngster's voice, and he dropped a hand to the pistol holstered on his right hip.

'I'll know the horse they were riding, and I'm gonna follow up that guy who rode off. He's carrying double. I ought to come up with him pretty soon. Your sister hired me on the spot, so I'm working for the Diamond O.'

'That's good news. I'll ride with you. I'd like to get

a bead on that back-shooting buzzard. Is my pa gonna live?'

'I think so.' Hilt nodded. 'But you better ride into town fast for the doctor. I'll track down those sidewinders. You split the breeze if you wanta save our father's life. He was bad hit.'

The youngster was thoughtful for a moment, then nodded and whirled his horse around to gallop after the buckboard. Hilt touched spurs to the buckskin and sent the big animal along the trail towards the fallen horse. He rode at a fast clip, and dismounted when he reached the dead animal. He gazed at the horse, shaking his head ruefully, then removed the saddle-bags from behind the cantle and squatted to check their contents. There was nothing in them by which to identify the rider and he straightened to check the tracks of the horse that had departed carrying double.

Mounting, he followed the tracks, pushing the buckskin into a run. His face was set grimly, for it looked as if, yet again, he was riding the gun trail despite his desire to lead a normal life.

He topped a rise and reined in quickly. The rider he was pursuing had dismounted halfway down the reverse slope and was squatting over the man Hilt had shot, who was sprawled on his back. Hilt slid his rifle out of its scabbard and cocked it. He fired a shot into the air and saw the man spring to his feet and swing around, his hand reaching for his holstered sixgun. Hilt fired again and dust spurted up an inch from the man's right boot, causing him to jump backwards.

The man turned and lunged for his horse. Hilt

fired yet again, aiming for the man's left shoulder, and started down the slope as the man staggered, then dropped to his knees before falling forward on to his face. Hilt slid his rifle into its boot and drew his pistol. He halted beside the two inert figures and dismounted, trailing his reins. Checking the men, he found that the man he had shot first was dead. The other was unconscious, his left shoulder dusted both sides.

Hilt dropped to one knee beside the wounded man and shook him by his uninjured shoulder. The man stirred and groaned and his eyelids flickered. Hilt holstered his gun and dragged the man into a sitting position, holding him upright as he sagged.

'Come on, wake up,' Hilt snapped.

The man groaned again and opened his eyes. He blinked rapidly, his gaze vacant until his senses returned fully. He looked at Hilt with narrowed, pain-filled eyes.

'Who in hell are you?' he demanded. 'Why'd you stick your nose in our business?'

'Who are you?' Hilt countered. 'Why were you shooting at the girl?'

'She wasn't the target. We was after Ormond.' The man groaned and slumped back, closing his eyes. 'You're in bad trouble, mister, sticking your nose in where it don't belong.'

'You're in worse trouble,' Hilt told him. 'Your pard is dead, and you're likely to bleed to death if I leave you here. So tell me what is going on and you just might save your life.'

'I ain't opening my trap about nothing.' The man

14

sighed and lost consciousness.

At that moment, Hilt heard a slight sound at his back and spun around, his hand darting to the butt of his holstered gun. A man was standing about ten feet away, holding a .45 in his right hand and looking as if he was ready to use the weapon. Hilt stayed his hand, his face expressionless as he faced the newcomer.

The man was middle-aged, wearing a light-blue store suit, white shirt and a black string tie. His feet were encased in expensive riding boots. Solid-looking, his face was fleshy, his features prominent; a long nose that was slightly bulbous at the end, flared nostrils, and a big chin rising towards his slit of a mouth. His forehead was wide, his grey eyes screwed up against the glare of the sun despite the shade afforded by his white Stetson, which was pulled down to within an inch of his bushy eyebrows. Sweat was beading his face and he looked uncomfortable in the heat, as if he were unaccustomed to being out in the sun. But the gun in his big paw of a hand was steady as a rock, its black muzzle pointing steadily at the centre of Hilt's chest.

'This is a mighty interesting situation.' The newcomer's voice was quiet and steady. 'What's going on?'

'It was even more interesting a while back,' Hilt said.

The man gave a white-toothed grin and nodded. 'Yeah. I heard the shooting. It looks like you're handling this so tell me what happened.'

'You sound like a lawman but I don't see a badge. So what's your interest?'

The man lifted his left hand and eased aside the lapel of his jacket. There was the glint of a sheriff's star that was pinned to the white shirt. 'I'm Rafe Catlin,' he said. 'Sheriff of Morgan County. Get on with it. What happened here?'

Hilt explained tersely and Catlin nodded, his levelled gun not wavering an inch. His weathered face was expressionless, his eyes narrowed and bright but giving no indication of what was passing through his mind. When Hilt fell silent, the sheriff moved to one side. Still covering Hilt carefully, he glanced at the two prostrate men.

'They're strangers to me,' he said. 'Ain't seen them around before. Or you either, come to that. The county is filling up with strangers, mostly gun-hung. You said Sue Ormond hired you?'

'That's a fact.'

'And what's your handle?'

'Frank Blaine.' Hilt used his mother's maiden name.

'Where'd you come from? You look like a long-rider.'

'I was working on the Bar 30 over Valverde way until a couple of weeks ago.' Hilt met the sheriff's gaze squarely.

Catlin shook his head. 'You don't look like a cowpoke. No sir! You ain't roped a steer in many a long day, if ever. I got you pegged for a gun-slammer, and there are too many of that breed riding into the county these days. So tell me what the attraction is?

Must mean trouble a'coming. You smokeroos gather where there's trouble like bees round a honey pot.'

'I ain't heard there's anything going on, and that's a fact. I'm riding the chuck line, aiming to work for my keep while looking for a permanent riding job, and happened to come on these two chasing and shooting at the Ormond buckboard. I stuck my nose in because there was a woman in the buckboard.'

'A noble reaction.' Catlin nodded his approval. 'You say you shot that one because he was shooting at the Ormonds. So what happened to this guy?'

Catlin nudged the unconscious man with the toe of his dusty riding boot.

'He tried to draw on me when I caught up with him, then tried to get away.'

'Uhuh. You reckon old man Ormond will live?'

'Yeah, if they get a sawbones to him mighty quick.'

'I'll give you the benefit of the doubt, Blaine, until I can check on your story.' Catlin holstered his gun with a slick movement. 'Throw that feller across his horse while I fetch my bronc and we'll ride into Diamond O. I don't like the sound of this business. Things have been threatening to bust out into open war, and if you're right then the smoke is giving way to fire.'

Hilt turned away and heaved the wounded man across his saddle. He swung into the hull and took hold of the reins of the watched the sheriff disappear into emerge moments later astride a allion that pulled, snorted and fought his rider all the way. When Catlin reined in beside Hilt the black tried to bite the neck of the buckskin and the sheriff hauled on his reins and forced the animal away.

'That's one mean piece of horseflesh,' Hilt commented.

'He fits in with most of the men who live hereabouts.' Catlin grinned. 'Are you leaving the corpse here?'

'Someone can pick him up later. He ain't gonna help your investigation none.'

The sheriff grimaced and fed steel to the black, which surged forward with powerful strides. Catlin turned his head and grinned at Hilt, then lifted a hand. 'I'll get on. See you at the Diamond O. I got a lot of ground to cover today and I don't want to waste time with the Ormonds.' He raked the black's flanks with his spurs and the animal departed fast, snorting and squealing.

Hilt rode steadily, leading the wounded man's horse. He wondered about the sheriff. The lawman seemed to be too casual about a situation that was building into a big problem. There was something seriously wrong on this range, and a sheriff worth his salt should be riding close herd on it, ready to act before the pot boiled over. Trouble on any range usually took the form of rustling, sheep, or someone trying to steal land, and Hilt wondered what it was here. The gun attack on the Ormonds was proof that lawlessness was erupting fast.

He rode steadily, keeping an eye on the wound man, and reined in when the inert figure slid off saddle and thudded on the hard ground. Dismounting, he went to the man's side and found him dead. He tut-tutted, hoisted the body back across the saddle and rode on.

Following the trail, he eventually came in sight of the distant ranch and looked around keenly as he approached. There were five figures standing on the porch of the ranch house, which stood apart from the other buildings, and they regarded him silently as he rode towards them. The sheriff was standing in the open doorway of the house, talking seriously to the intent men, but Catlin lapsed into silence when Hilt rode within earshot. The men were cowhands, and Hilt recognized one of them as the ranch foreman, who had driven the buckboard on to the ranch.

Hilt dismounted and wrapped his reins around a convenient hitching rail, his gaze intent upon the men, looking for a familiar face. But these were strangers, and he saw raw suspicion on each hard countenance. No one spoke, and Hilt nodded to himself as he removed his Stetson to beat it against his left thigh.

'Why do I feel like a snake that's crawled into the church on a Sunday?' he commented.

'We don't take kindly to a stranger who sticks his nose into our business,' growled Art Weston. The foreman strode to the edge of the porch and scowled at Hilt, his hard brown eyes filled with smouldering distrust. Seen up close, he was thin-lipped, burly and hard-bitten. Dressed in dusty range clothes, he looked tough and arrogant. Hilt gained the impression that he was a man of wicked temper.

'You reckon I should have sat on that ridge and watched the shooting without butting in, huh?' Hilt shook his head. 'I saw a woman in the buckboard, and that was enough to trigger me, I reckon.' He glanced around at the watchful men. 'In my boots, how many of you would have stayed out of it?'

Catlin left the doorway and came to the edge of the porch, standing nonchalantly at Weston's side. 'Don't get the wrong slant on this, Blaine,' he advised. 'You did good by horning in, and Sue will put out the welcome sign for you when she gets around to it.' He glanced at the assembled men. 'Take a look at that galoot across the saddle and see if any of you can put a name to him. He was shooting at your boss.'

Hilt watched the cowhands crowd around the lead horse. Art Weston grasped hold of the dead man's hair and twisted the face around so they could see it. After a moment the waddies backed off, shaking their heads and murmuring negatively. Weston let go of the head and rubbed his hand against his thigh. His face was set in deep creases that accentuated his age.

'You got more business here?' he demanded, facing Hilt, his right hand edging towards the butt of his holstered .45.

'Sure have.' Hilt's dark gaze bored into the ramrod's slitted eyes.

'I run this outfit and I ain't hiring, if that's in your mind.' Weston spat out the words and, when Hilt grinned, the ramrod's cheeks became tinged with a dull red flush. A murderous glint fanned to life in the depths of his eyes. His thin lips parted, but then he changed his mind and moistened them, at the same time lifting his left hand to thumb back the black Stetson from his rugged forehead. 'You better fork your bronc and split the breeze out of here,' he grated. 'Get to hell and gone. We don't need your kind on Diamond O.'

'Too bad!' There was studied insolence in Hilt's tone and his chill brown eyes filled with unmistakable challenge. 'You don't get up early enough in the mornings, mister, to keep up with events. I'm hired already.'

'Is that so?' Weston pushed back his wide shoulders. 'Sure, I know what the lady said, but she was shocked and didn't know what she was saying. Now, if you know what's good for you, get to hell out of here.'

'And if I don't?' Hilt was pushing the man to his limit.

Weston grinned wickedly, and Hilt matched him, showing his teeth in a soundless smile. Hilt wanted to see which way the ramrod would jump. If trouble was eating up this ranch then it pointed to the fact that the ramrod was not doing his job properly.

'Don't make trouble for yourself,' Weston snarled. 'You got the look of a man who knows a thing or two, but I'll spell it for you: you ain't wanted here and it's my job to move you on. So make up your mind. Leave on your own account or get busted up before I throw you off the ranch. It's your choice, mister.'

Hilt stepped back a pace to bring all the men into plain view, his right hand hanging limply by his side. His body seemed to sag a little and his shoulders settled slightly forward.

'That's fighting talk, mister,' he rapped, and waited patiently for Weston's reaction. . . .

TWO

The silence that ensued after Hilt's challenge was fraught with menace. Weston stiffened and his right hand edged closer to the butt of his gun, his fingers twitching slightly. His eyes were like those of a bull, reddened with natural fury, and his thin lips took on a fixed smile. But the sheriff moved first. A long stride brought him over the edge of the porch and he stepped down into the dust to stand between Weston and Hilt, his right palm pressing against the ramrod's big chest.

'Just take it easy, the pair of you,' he said smoothly. 'Everyone here's got the interests of Diamond O at heart. Blaine has just killed two men for the brand, and probably saved Sue from taking a slug. If anyone can beat that score then go ahead and brace Blaine.'

Hilt met Weston's gaze, grinned maliciously, and saw the flame in the ramrod's eyes intensify. He was aware that Weston had reached his limit. But even as he gauged the big man's attitude, he saw the fire die from Weston's eyes. The ramrod heaved a sigh and tension seeped out of him.

'If Sue hired you then you better stick around,' he said grudgingly, his face suddenly expressionless. He rounded on the watching cowpokes. 'What in hell are you standing around for?' he demanded. 'Is this what you get paid for? Bland, hit your saddle and ride over to Mulejaw Creek. Check that nobody has moved in on the water.' He paused and glanced at the silent Catlin. 'Mebbe this is what it's all about, Sheriff. We got word last week that an outfit was fixing to move in on our water. They could be doing that right now, while we're distracted by the shooting here.'

'You got any idea who is likely to move in?' Catlin demanded. 'I don't see a local outfit trying it.'

'If I knew their identity they would have been planted by now. But we'll get to them when they make their move.' Weston left the porch and strode away without another glance at Hilt.

'I wonder what's eating him?' mused the sheriff. 'He sounds like he swallowed a mouse and gulped a rat to catch it. Art ain't never been a placid man, but right now he sure is riled up about something. Mebbe that attack on Chuck and Sue upset him. He sure thinks the sun shines outa that gal.'

'How is the boss?' Hilt demanded.

'I took a look at him. I reckon he'll live.' Catlin nodded. 'Young Billy lit out for town to fetch Doc Errol. I hope you make out all right around here, Blaine. But by the looks of it, Weston is gonna give you a hard time.'

24

'He don't worry me none.' Hilt smiled. ' I reckon he's out of his depth in this situation and is likely to change his mind about me when he sees how I can help out.'

'You've got it all to do.' Catlin prepared to move out. 'When you get to town, drop into my office to make a statement about what happened when those two hardcases started shooting at the Ormonds. For the record, you understand.'

'I'll do that.' Hilt stepped on to the porch as the sheriff departed and sat down on a chair beside the open front door. He tilted his hat over his eyes and relaxed. But almost immediately he sensed that he was not alone, and arose quickly, his gaze falling upon Sue Ormond, who was standing motionless in the doorway, her face marred by worry, her eyes haunted by shock. Her right hand was resting on the butt of a .38 pistol holstered on her hip.

'So you caught up with those men!' She suppressed a shudder as her gaze encompassed the inert figure draped across the saddle of the horse at the tie rail. 'Did you have to kill him? Wouldn't it have been better to take him prisoner and try to learn why he attacked us?'

'I tried to do that.' Hilt spoke quietly. 'But he had other ideas about it so I tried for a wing shot, but he was moving fast and I had to get him the best way I could. I didn't want him to get away.'

'So you have no idea who he is or why he was shooting at my father and me?'

'None at all, and he's a stranger to your crew. They've looked him over.'

'I've told Art Weston about you.' She moved out of the doorway and looked around the yard. 'Art is the foreman here. He's against hiring gunmen on principle, but the good of the ranch comes first with him, and although he's a difficult man to work with, you should get along with him. He'll accept you when he sees what an asset you are.'

'I've already met him.' Hilt nodded. 'We'll rub along all right.'

'Good.' She looked at him with sparkling eyes. 'I shall never be able to thank you enough for saving Father and me. I dread to think what might have happened if you hadn't bought into it when you did.'

He grinned. 'I'm sure glad I showed up in time. What do you have in mind for me to do around here?'

She seemed undecided for a moment, and Hilt could feel the power of her pale gaze upon him. She seemed utterly defenceless and alone, and he had to make a deliberate effort to suppress the strand of emotion that tried to unwind in his breast. A tremoring thrill passed through him as he considered, and he firmly dismissed the common-sense thought that he should ride out fast and shake the dust of this range off his boots. His experience warned that nothing but trouble could come from sticking around.

'In view of what happened this afternoon, I think you should stick close to me wherever I go.' Sue drew a deep breath and restrained it for a moment while she considered. 'Someone is out to take Diamond O from us. That much is certain. There have been several incidents pointing to the fact, but until today my father has chosen to ignore the signs. No doubt, if he lives through this, what happened this afternoon will certainly change his mind.' Her soft voice faltered and she clenched her hands, making a visible effort to control herself. 'Your job will be to protect us from further attack. I'm sure this trouble can only get worse, and I want to be prepared for it.'

Hilt was watching the activity across the yard. The sheriff, over by the corral, was talking seriously to Art Weston, and the big ramrod's attitude indicated resentment. Weston shook his head vigorously and turned away from the lawman, who stepped up into his saddle and rode off towards the gate while Weston came back to the house, stamping through the thick dust of the yard.

'I'll get myself a bed in the bunkhouse and put my gear away,' Hilt observed. 'Then I'll be ready to take up my duties.'

'That won't do.' Sue's tone sharpened. 'How could you protect us at night if you're sleeping in the bunkhouse? There's a room for you here in the house, and you'd better sleep with one eye open. Bring your gear in and I'll show you where to stow it.'

Hilt thumbed the brim of his Stetson back off his forehead and went to his horse, removing his bedroll and slicker from behind the cantle. As he stepped on to the porch again, Weston arrived. The ramrod called to the girl as she entered the house, and she paused and turned to face him, showing defiance.

'You ain't having him sleep in the house, Sue,' Weston snapped. 'It ain't right, and you must be plumb loco. We don't know a thing about him. He could even be one of that bunch out to get us.'

'Don't be absurd,' she rapped. 'Blaine saved Father and me this afternoon. I've listened to you for the last time, Art. This morning I wanted one of the men to ride with us into town and you said you couldn't spare anyone. So what is more important around here, the ranch chores or our lives? You get back to your work, Art, and leave this business to me, I'm taking control of the ranch while Father is indisposed. Come on, Blaine. I'll show you to your room.'

Hilt looked into Weston's eyes as he entered the house behind the girl, and his grin was intended to set the ramrod's blood pressure soaring.

'You think you're smart, mister,' Weston rapped. 'But I'll be watching you every minute. Don't ever put a foot wrong.'

Hilt followed the girl into the house and they ascended a wide staircase. A passage ran the length of the upper storey, with doors opening off on either side. The first door on the right stood open and Hilt glanced into the bedroom in passing. He saw Chuck Ormond lying on the bed, stripped to the waist and with his shoulder heavily bandaged. A middle-aged, grey-haired woman was bending over him. When he paused, Sue Ormond came back to him.

'Dad's in a bad way,' she said uncertainly, and the woman beside the bed glanced in their direction. 'That's Helen tending him. She's been our house-keeper since my mother died.' She sighed heavily. 'I fear my father will not survive this.'

'He looks tough enough to pull through.' Hilt spoke with a confidence he did not feel. 'You can bet your boots that he'll make it.'

She smiled wanly and went on, showing him into a small room at the end of the passage that over-looked the back of the house.

'This sure looks better than the bunkhouse,' he observed, moving to the small window and peering out across the back of the house. The ground had been cleared of vegetation for a distance of fifty yards, and Hill nodded, relieved that someone was alert to the dangers facing the ranch. He inspected the room. It was clean, although sparsely furnished. Dumping his gear on the bed, he turned to speak to Sue but the sound of galloping hoofs alerted him and he hurried from the room, crossed the passage and entered a room opposite that overlooked the front yard.

As he bent to peer out of the window a fusillade of shots shattered the silence, and he heard the deadly thud of hot lead striking the front of the house. He ducked when a bullet shattered the window, and grasped Sue as she entered the room, pushing her to the floor. She gazed up at him with fear showing starkly in her eyes.

'What's happening?' she gasped.

'Stay put while I find out.' He drew his gun, ran to the stairs, and descended them two at a time.

Gunfire was booming outside, mingled with the sound of pounding hoofs. Hilt cocked his gun and crossed to the window beside the front door. Peering out, he saw half-a-dozen riders galloping around the yard, trading lead with the Diamond O crew, who had dropped into defensive positions. He saw Art Weston crouched by the corral, shooting rapidly at the riders.

Hilt opened the front door and immediately drew fire from two riders to his left, who were evidently watching the house. He lifted his gun and fired without seeming to take aim, and one of the two men pitched out of leather and fell on his face in the dust. The second man spurred his horse forward, shooting as he came, riding his horse straight at the porch. Hilt shot him out of the saddle.

'Who are those men?' demanded Sue, coming to Hilt's side.

'Get into cover,' he rapped, and went outside to the porch, his keen gaze taking in the positions of the attacking men.

His gun flamed and a rider in the act of overrunning Weston's position flung up his arms and pitched out of his saddle. Hilt moved to the end of the porch overlooking the bunkhouse. Two riders were coming towards him from that direction and he dropped to one knee as slugs thudded into the woodwork close to him. He felt the tug of a bullet passing through the crown of his Stetson and fired instantly in reply. His first shot struck the right-hand man, his second tearing through the face of the other. Both men fell in a tangle while their horses ran on, and Hilt cuffed back his Stetson, filled with swiftly mounting anger as he wiped his sweating forehead with his sleeve.

The shooting was fading away and Hilt looked

around, deadly gun uplifted. One rider was galloping out through the gateway, raising dust as he split
the breeze. Hilt relaxed and reloaded his smoking
weapon. Gun echoes were fading into the distance,
and he glanced around when he heard a sound at his
back. Sue was standing in the doorway of the house,
her face pale and shock clearly apparent in her eyes.

'What on earth is happening?' she demanded.
'Who are those men? Is the sheriff still here?'

Hilt glanced around. The cowhands were emerging from cover, all holding guns. Art Weston was
coming towards the house, reloading his gun, his
fleshy face grim and angry.

'Mebbe Weston can tell us who these men are.'
Hilt finished reloading his gun and slid it into his
holster. He leaned a shoulder against the front wall
of the house, watching the big ramrod's approach.

'Are you all right, Sue?' Weston demanded.
'Nobody got into the house, huh?'

'Thanks to Blaine, they didn't,' she replied. 'He
knocked down at least five of those riders. You got
any idea who they are, Art?'

'I've told the boys to gather them together and
check them out,' Weston's voice grated angrily. He
cuffed back his Stetson and wiped sweat from his
forehead 'It'll be the last time anyone will be able to
ride into this yard, I can tell you.'

'Is the sheriff still here?' Sue asked, and sighed
when Weston shook his head.

'He's coming in now,' Hilt observed. 'He must
have heard the shooting.'

Catlin was approaching the gate at a fast clip, and

he came to the porch before reining in and looking around the yard at the sprawled figures. The Diamond O crew were placing the dead men in a row in front of the bunkhouse.

'I heard the shooting and couldn't believe it,' Catlin said. 'It sounded like a real battle.'

'It was while it lasted,' Sue retorted. She shook her head, still badly shocked. 'It's like a nightmare. First Dad and I were shot at, now this.'

'I'll take a look at the bodies, ' Catlin turned his horse and rode across the yard with Weston following closely.

'Someone sure is set on causing trouble for Diamond O,' Hilt observed. 'Have any of your neighbours been giving you trouble? What was it I heard about someone planning to take over your water? Mulejaw Creek, isn't it? Weston mentioned it earlier.'

'There was some talk going around earlier in the week.' Sue drew a deep breath and held it for a moment before sighing heavily. 'One of the men heard something about it in town. We've been keeping watch, but nothing happened until today.'

'And now we're up to our necks in trouble.' Hilt was watching the sheriff and the ramrod as they examined the line of dead men. 'How long has Catlin been the sheriff around here?' he queried. 'I don't like the way he rode out just before that bunch came in, and then showed up again afterwards.'

'He's been the sheriff about two years. Old Sheriff Benton was killed in a shoot-out when the bank was robbed. Catlin had not long taken a job as a deputy when it happened, and he stepped into Benton's boots when nobody else wanted the job. But surely the sheriff is above suspicion, isn't he?'

'Who knows?' Hilt shrugged. 'Especially when no one seems able to put a name to even one of the raiders.'

Catlin came back to the porch, dismounted and tied his black to the rail. He pushed back the brim of his Stetson. 'This is the hell of a note,' he said, shaking his head. 'We got seven dead men and three bad wounded down in the dust, and they're all strangers. Leastways, nobody admits to seeing any of them before. It's a good thing you showed up when you did, Blaine. Seems like you killed most of those hardcases. The way Weston described it, that was some shooting. You're mighty slick with that gun of yours. We got two or three gunnies in the county, but I doubt if any of them is in your class.' He grinned but his eyes remained coldly analytical. 'You wanted by the law anywhere?'

'Not that I know of.' Hilt smiled. 'I never hire out my gun. I came in here to get a riding job.'

'And that's out of the question,' said Sue. 'I want you to stick close to the house after this. Sheriff, if you see any gunhands around the county who are looking for a job then send them on here.'

'It won't do to start hiring guns,' Catlin warned.

'We would be in a poor way now if Blaine hadn't shown up when he did,' Sue retorted. 'Don't try to tell me what I should or should not do, Sheriff. I know enough about the ways of this country to know what I'm talking about, and the only thing to do when strangers come riding and shooting into your yard is have a crew that's strong enough to stop them dead in their tracks.'

'Well you surely did that,' Catlin observed.

'Have you checked out the horses that were downed, Sheriff?' Hilt asked. 'Mebbe one of them is carrying a local brand. That might help you locate the place where the riders came from.'

Catlin shook his head. 'I've looked them over and none of them is carrying any sign. That tells me a lot. Someone is taking great pains to conceal their identity.' He turned and looked around the yard. 'I got to be riding. Art is gonna load all the bodies in the buckboard and send them into town. I'll be checking out this business, don't you fret, Sue. Leave it to me. So long, Blaine. I don't think anything will go wrong around here while you're on the spread.'

Catlin jerked his reins free from the rail and swung into his saddle. The black lunged forward and tried to bite Weston as he approached but the ramrod was alert to the animal's tricks and avoided it. Catlin lifted a hand and departed at a canter. They watched him in silence until he disappeared beyond a distant rise, leaving just a thin plume of dust to mark his passing.

'Where is Cedar Creek from here?' Hilt enquired.

'The trail leads straight to town,' Sue told him. 'It's about twelve miles from here. I do hope Billy will be all right. We should have sent a man with him, Art.'

'Too late now to worry about that,' Weston

34

retorted. 'But Billy can take care of himself, and he'll be primed for trouble.'

'You'll have to manage without me for a spell,' Hilt said. 'There's something I have to do.'

'I won't feel safe if you ride out,' Sue said in alarm. 'Can't your business wait?'

Hilt shook his head. 'It's your business not mine, and I can't leave it. Nobody has got a line on these raiders, and I have a feeling that Catlin won't accomplish much. But there are tracks out there that will lead right to the place those men came from. It should be easy to trail a bunch of horses, and I'd also like to trail the two men who ambushed you back to where they started out. We need to know if both groups came from the same place.'

'Can't you leave that to Art and the crew?' Sue asked.

'Sure I could. But I'd like to handle it myself. I won't trust anyone else to do it.' Hilt met the ramrod's hard gaze as he spoke, and grinned when the man bristled angrily. 'If I get this right then we could have the answer to your problems before the day is out, so I won't waste time. I'm riding now.'

'All right.' Sue nodded but her face was showing reluctance. 'I don't think anything more will happen today. But come back as soon as you can, won't you?'

'You can bet on it.' Hilt went into the house to fetch his gear. He returned to the porch and tied his blanket roll behind the cantle, then mounted. 'I'll be as quick as I can.' He lifted a hand in farewell and rode across the yard, dismounting in the gateway to study tracks. He saw where at least nine horses had

35

approached in a bunch, noted the characteristics of some of the hoof-prints, and mounted to set off at a canter, his keen gaze watching the tracks.

He checked his surroundings from time to time, aware of the dangers in riding along tracks where a man might be waiting beside the trail for just such a probability. He had travelled some three miles, heading south-west, when he spotted the tracks of a single horse joining the trail he was following, coming in from his right, and he recalled the rider who had high-tailed it from Diamond O after the shooting. The rider was moving fast, judging by the tracks, and Hilt pushed on grimly, wanting some answers to the questions prominent in his mind.

Hilt's thoughts were meandering over the broad face of the situation. As far as he was concerned it would be a simple matter to locate those responsible for the trouble at Diamond O. He thought of Sue Ormond, and knew that he could not turn his back on her. He was hooked, whether he liked it or not, and his own quest - hunting down Buck Dunne - would have to wait until he had unravelled this local issue.

The afternoon was well advanced when the tracks he was following veered to his left, leaving a single set of tracks still going on. He reined in, knowing that he had to be close to Cedar Creek and certain that the single tracks belonged to the rider who had escaped from the shooting at Diamond O.

Looking around, he spotted a thin spiral of smoke rising into the sky in the direction the single rider had taken. He rode to the nearest rise and saw, just ahead, a line shack beside a narrow stream. Two horses were standing hip-shot in the shade of a nearby clump of trees, but there was no sign of human life. He rode down the slope without hesitation and reined in before the open doorway of the shack.

'Anyone to home?' he called, and heard his voice echo in the heavy silence. He sat easy in the saddle, hands in plain view on the saddlehorn.

'What's your business?' a hoarse voice demanded from inside the shack. 'Don't make any sudden moves, mister. I got a gun on you.'

'I'm passing through and need to water my horse,' Hilt replied.

'Go ahead and do it, then get outa here.'

'Thanks.' Hilt turned his horse towards the stream and dismounted, his gaze surveying the area. He thought he saw a movement at the window of the shack but could not be sure, and stood watching the buckskin while it drank. He did not show any undue interest in the shack, but looked over the horses tethered in the shade, ensuring that he would know them again. When the buckskin had taken its fill he swung into the saddle and rode off, lifting a hand and waving farewell. He did not look back.

As soon as he was lost to sight of the shack, Hilt dismounted and took his field-glasses from the saddle-bag. Leaving the horse in cover, he dropped to the ground and eased forward until he could see the front of the ramshackle building. A man was standing in the doorway, holding a rifle ready for action and looking around suspiciously. Hilt studied him through the glasses. He saw a heavily bearded face and decided that the man had not been one of the Diamond O raiders.

But there were two horses in the shade, and Hilt wondered if a second man was in the shack. He returned to the buckskin, led the animal deeper into cover, then set out on foot to check the shack. He went to the left, staying under cover, and reached the rear of the building without incident. A heavy silence was broken only by the faint murmuring of the nearby stream.

Hilt reached the back of the cabin. There was a rear door, which was closed. He found a knot-hole in a plank and applied an eye to it. The interior of the single room was dim but he saw the bearded man talking to another who was seated at a rough table, his shirt, stained with blood, open to the waist.

Without hesitation, Hilt drew his .45 and walked around the shack. He entered the doorway with his gun levelled, and the bearded man lunged sideways to pick up his rifle, which was leaning against the table. Hilt fired a shot that shattered the man's outstretched left hand. The crash of the detonation reverberated in the close confines of the shack and gunsmoke plumed across the room, stinging Hilt's nostrils. The bearded man dropped to the floor, twisting to face Hilt, and reached desperately for the pistol holstered on his right hip. His eyes were narrowed, his mouth agape, and desperation was showing in his narrowed gaze.

'Leave it be,' Hilt warned.

The man stayed his hand at the last moment, fingers just touching the butt of his weapon. His bearded face gave no clue to his intention and Hilt's trigger finger tremored, on the brink of sending the man to hell. The man heaved a long sigh and then moved his right hand from the proximity of his gun and grasped his shattered left hand. Blood was dripping copiously from the wound.

'That's better.' Hilt stepped in close and snaked the man's pistol from its holster. He looked at the second man, who had frozen at his entrance. 'The last time I saw you, you were riding out of the Diamond O with hot lead crackling around you, and it looks like you stopped a slug for your trouble. So, now you can do some talking. Who are you, and what's going on around Diamond O? Give it to me straight or I'll finish you so fast you'll be in Hell before you can blink. You're standing on the brink right now, mister, and there's only one way you can save your hide, so start talking.'

'I don't know what you're talking about.' The man shook his head. 'I'm a Big D cowhand. This is a Big D line camp. I'm Tom Pilk. I was shot in town last night and only just got away from the sheriff. We figured you was one of a posse after me.'

'You're a liar! ' Hilt spoke harshly. 'I saw you at Diamond O earlier. Now come up with the truth. I ain't got time for fooling around so spill it, or take it with you to Boot Hill.'

THREE

Only the buzzing of a fly in the close confines of the cabin marred the deathly silence. Hilt watched the two men, who were staring grimly at him. The bearded man was gripping his shattered left hand, his lips compressed against the pain of the wound. Pilk shook his head, defiance showing in his gaze.

'You got five seconds to start talking, or I'll kill you,' Hilt moved the muzzle of his gun until the muzzle pointed between Pilk' s eyes. 'I'm on the Diamond O payroll as a gun hand, and I'm just doing my job, so let's get to it. The five seconds start now.'

He lapsed into silence. To Pilk, the muzzle of the gun seemed to grow larger until it looked the size of a cannon. He moistened his lips, still hesitant to talk.

'Five!' Hilt rapped.

'Hold it.' Desperation sounded in Pilk's voice. 'I'm trying to think it over.'

'You don't need to think about what you're doing.' Hilt smiled. 'You said you're riding for Big D; why are they hiring two-bit gunnies?'

'There's big trouble coming.' Pilk spat out the words as if they were burning his mouth. 'All the ranchers are hiring gunmen.'

'So who ordered you and those others to attack Diamond O? And what do you know about the two men who shot at the Ormonds before the rest of you rode into the ranch like a pack of redskins?'

'My boss, Frank Downey, sent us out on the gun trail.' Pilk pressed a hand to his upper chest, where blood was staining his shirt. 'There's been rustling on the range, and we got the word that Diamond O is responsible for it. The sheriff has done nothing about the stealing so we had to handle it.'

'I don't believe Chuck Ormond is a rustler.' Hilt laughed harshly. 'You'll have to do better than that, mister. Give it to me straight. Or do you reckon I won't shoot you?'

He fired a shot, aiming for the crown of Pilk's Stetson. The hat jerked and Pilk flinched, his eyes widening as the crash of the shot filled the cabin. He ducked, and fell sideways off his chair. Hilt recocked his gun and stood with the muzzle upraised.

'So that was the plan, huh?' Hilt demanded. 'Two of your bunch attacked the Ormonds, and then the rest of you rode into the ranch to take over.'

Pilk looked up from the dirt floor, his face grey, his eyes showing fear. 'I don't know anything about that,' he muttered. 'I just obey orders.'

'Now we're getting somewhere.' Hilt grinned. 'So who gave the orders?'

'Chain Hindle, the Big D foreman. He told Hap Arlot, the gun boss, what to do, and Arlot worked out the best way to do it.'

'That's better.' Hilt came to a decision. 'On your feet. I'm taking you back to Diamond O. You were the only one to ride out of the Ormond ranch, Pilk, so I got the feeling that Big D has lost its gun crew. Get up, and let's go.' He glanced at the other man, who had remained silent. 'What's your name?'

'Jake Cottrill. I don't know a thing about any shooting. I'm a ranch hand. I've been at this line camp more than two weeks, on the watch for rustlers, and I ain't seen hide nor hair of a single soul until Pilk rode in a short time ago. I ain't in this trouble, and if I leave here I'll get fired.'

'You're riding to Diamond O with us, Cottrill. Go and get your horses ready to travel, and don't try anything.'

Both men left the cabin and Hilt followed closely. Pilk staggered, and leaned against the front wall of the cabin. Hilt moved in on him as Cottrill went to the horses and began saddling the animals. Hilt examined Pilk's wound, which was not serious.

'You'll do,' he said unfeelingly. 'It ain't serious. The bleeding has stopped.'

'I need to see a doctor,' Pilk retorted.

'There should be one at Diamond O by the time we get there. Chuck Ormond is hurt bad, and the rest of the bunch you rode into the ranch with were down in the dust when I left. Most of them looked dead to me. You're the lucky one, Pilk. I reckon you just might come out of this alive, if you use your brains.'

Pilk received the grim news in silence, and

moments later, after Hilt had bound the hands of both men and tied the bridles of their mounts together, they were riding out. Hilt collected the buckskin and rode behind his prisoners. They travelled at a canter through the late afternoon, back towards the Diamond O. Hilt stayed a couple of yards behind his prisoners, his deadly gun now in its holster. His watchful gaze regarded his surroundings as they travelled.

Evening was well advanced when they came in sight of the Diamond O, and Hilt's eyes glinted when he saw the ranch-house lamps shining through the gathering twilight. He glanced around. Nothing stirred on the surrounding range and the silence was intense, but when they reached the gateway to the yard a voice called a challenge.

'Frank Blaine with a couple of prisoners,' he replied, and a man emerged from the blackness beyond the gate, rifle in hand.

'Are they two of the skunks who was shooting at us earlier?' the guard demanded.

'One of them is,' Hilt said. 'Has the doctor showed up?'

'Yeah, and he's still here. The good news is that the boss is gonna pull through. But two of those gunnies we downed have cashed in their chips. We got one prisoner left from that bunch. Who you got there? Do I know them?'

'Pilk and Cottrill. They reckon they ride for Big D.'

'Is Downey back of this trouble? Heck, it wouldn't surprise me if he is. He sure runs a salty crew. They've caused plenty of trouble around the county.'

'What kind of trouble?' Hilt enquired.

'Fighting in town and shooting on the range. They reckon they lost more stock to rustlers than the rest of us put together.'

'I reckon we'll get to the bottom of it now. Pilk, lead the way to the house. You know where it is.'

'There'll be another guard on the porch,' he was warned.

When they reached the ranch-house a vague figure emerged from the shadows of the veranda and a challenge reached out softly. Hilt identified himself, and as he stepped down from his saddle, Sue Ormond spoke from the open doorway of the house.

'I'm glad you're back, Blaine. I've been worried about you. Did you have any trouble out there?'

'Not that you'd notice. I got a couple of prisoners, and what they admit to is mighty interesting. But they need questioning by the law to get at the truth. I'm a stranger hereabouts, with no local knowledge, so I don't know what to believe.'

'Who are they?' Art Weston' s growling tone came out of the darkness from the end of the porch. 'I didn't expect to see you back, Blaine. You're full of surprises. So you got lucky, huh? Well I'll get the truth out of them. Where did you find them?'

'At the Big D line shack.'

'The hell you say! I've had my suspicions of Big D.' Weston stamped across the porch and peered at the two men, who were faintly visible in the light coming from the nearest window. 'Yeah, I've seen them around. Patton, take them over to the corral and get them outa their saddles. We'll talk to them over there.'

The guard grasped the reins of the two horses and led them away, Weston following closely, and Hilt wrapped his reins around the tie rail and looked up at Sue Ormond's slim figure silhouetted on the porch by the light issuing through a window.

'The guard told me your father will pull through,' he said.

'Yes.' Her voice was thick with emotion. 'I'm mighty grateful for the way you showed up at just the right time. Doc Errol is still here. He's only just finished treating my father.'

'So everything is all right,' Hilt observed.

'Not really.' Her voice faltered. 'My brother Billy didn't come back with the doctor. He stayed in town with the idea of trying to learn something. But, knowing him, all he's likely to do is find trouble. Cedar Creek is a tough place these days.'

Hilt nodded. 'Yeah,' he mused. 'I got the idea, looking at your brother earlier, that he's kind of hot-blooded. You think he might find trouble in town?'

'I'm sure of it. And if anything happened to Billy, it would finish my father. Would you go to town and bring him back?'

Hilt laughed harshly. 'I'm prepared to nurse cows,' he said, 'but I don't expect to mother a wild-eyed kid. And he sure wouldn't appreciate me going into town to fetch him back.'

'I'll ride in with you,' she said worriedly. 'If whoever is causing this trouble is prepared to shoot Father and me, then I'm sure he wouldn't hesitate to kill Billy if he got the chance, would he?'

'I guess you're right. It's a pity you didn't send one of the crew for the doctor and kept your brother where you could see him. Sure, I'll ride into town, but you'd better stay here. I don't need you to distract me, and you'll be safer here with the crew around you. They seem to be on their toes now. But I don't reckon you'll have any more trouble at the moment.'

'My father said he would like to see you when you showed up.' She stepped into the house and Hilt followed closely. They entered a big sitting-room. The interior was lit dimly, and a figure moved forward from the rear of the room. Hilt caught a faint smell of cooked food, which reminded him that he was ravenous.

'I've got a meal ready for you,' the housekeeper said quietly. 'Shall I serve it now?'

'Sure thing.' Hilt nodded. 'I could eat a horse,'

'We prefer beef,' the woman countered, and Hilt laughed.

'I'll take him up to see Father, Helen, ' Sue said. 'You can feed him shortly.'

Hilt followed the girl up the stairs and into her father's bedroom. The rancher was lying propped up in bed. The lantern on a bedside table was turned up high, filling the room with yellow brilliance. A tall, thin man, probably in his sixties, with greying hair brushed back from a high forehead, was putting surgical instruments into a black medical bag, and he paused when Sue Ormond introduced Hilt, his keen blue eyes glinting behind spectacles.

'Doc Errol, meet Frank Blaine,' Sue said.

'Mighty glad to make your acquaintance, Blaine, ' Errol said, in a quiet, precise tone, and held out his hand. 'You saved Chuck's life.'

'Howdy, Doc.' Hilt shook hands briefly. 'I happened to be in the right place at the right time, that's all.'

Sue continued, 'Dad, this is Frank Blaine, the man who saved both our lives, and then shot most of those raiders who showed up later.'

Chuck Ormond held out an unsteady hand, a wide smile on his pale features. 'Son, I'm glad to know you.' He spoke in a firm voice. He was a big-framed man but gaunt from a lifetime of too much saddle-work. His blue eyes were steady as Hilt clasped his hand briefly. 'I'd like to thank you for what you did. You sure saved my life and, what is more, you saved Sue from bad trouble. You've got a job on Diamond O for as long as you want it, and if there's ever anything I can do for you then just ask, huh?'

'Thanks.' Hilt nodded. 'I guess anyone would have butted in when they saw a girl being shot at.'

'There are some rough men in the county these days,' Doc Errol observed. 'The signs are mighty bad. I travel around a lot, and I don't like what I see. It's getting too bad for women and children to live in safety, and God knows how it will end. I reckon there'll be a great demand for my services before it's through.'

'I'd like some time off right now,' Hilt said. 'I need to ride into town and look around. I'm too much of a

47

stranger to be much use to you. I reckon to hit town, get my bearings, and be back here come sun-up.'

'Sure thing.' Chuck Ormond nodded. 'Take as much time as you need. We're on our guard now, and I don't think there'll be any more gunnies riding in to shoot us up.'

'We can ride together. I'm almost ready to go back to town,' Doc Errol said, 'and I'd be glad of some company. Maybe I can give you some pointers on what's happening around here. I see a lot in my travels.'

'I need to eat before I ride out,' Hilt said. 'I'll be ready in about fifteen minutes.'

Chuck Ormond was studying Hilt shrewdly. 'If you see Billy around town when you get there perhaps you'll tell him I want him back here pronto, huh?'

'Sure. I'll keep an eye open for him.' Hilt grinned.

'I heard that you and Art don't see eye to eye,' Ormond continued. 'He's a strange man is Art, but one of the best, and he'd lay down his life for the brand. He certainly knows his business. But he's tough when it comes to strangers riding in. He ain't got an ounce of trust in him. If I was to hand out advice about working with Art, I'd say you'd have to make the effort to get along with him. He wouldn't meet you halfway.'

'I got great respect for men who can run a cattle spread,' Hilt said. 'And I can get along with most men. Now I'd better get moving. The sooner I leave, the sooner I'll get back.'

Sue led him back down the stairs and through to

the kitchen, where a large plate piled high with good-smelling food was on the table. The girl departed quietly as he sat down at the table and fell to eating without hesitation. The housekeeper remained nearby, greatly pleased and smiling benignly at the pleasure which Hilt displayed in her cooking.

Hilt felt ready to face what lay before him by the time he had cleared the plate. He dipped a home-made biscuit into the rich gravy, ate it, and sighed contentedly. Helen brought a pot from the stove and he drank two cups of coffee, lingering over the second. Then he arose quickly, murmuring his thanks for the meal. He could hear the doctor's voice in the hall, and went through to find Sue with Errol, who was waiting to leave.

'I aim to be back by sun-up,' Hilt told Sue. 'I don't expect anything to happen before then.'

'I doubt if I shall be able to sleep tonight,' she replied. 'I have a feeling that I ought to confide in you; at least give you some idea of the problems facing us.'

'That can wait until I get back,' he decided. 'Another night shouldn't make much difference.'

'You should be made aware of who will be friendly towards you in town, and who might not,' she persisted.

'Don't worry about it.' Hilt grinned. 'I regard all strangers as unfriendly. See you in the morning. Are you ready to ride, Doc?'

'I sure am. I got a couple of patients waiting to be seen in town. So long, Sue. Try not to worry about

49

what's going on. You and Chuck were lucky today, and I hope that luck will hold through the near future.'

'Thank you for coming so promptly,' she replied.

Hilt went out to the buckskin, and paused when he saw that the animal had been taken away. A fine-looking roan was standing in its place, and Art Weston was sitting on the porch seat. The ramrod got to his feet when Hilt emerged from the house and came to confront him.

'I figure your buckskin needs a rest,' Weston growled. 'You can borrow my roan. He'll run for ever, if needs be. Treat him right and he won't let you down. When you get to town you better watch out for any Big D crew. And there's a man called Ben Hussey who fancies himself as a gun slammer. He hangs out in the Black Ace saloon; a gambler with a nasty habit of calling out strangers who look like they might be riding the gun trail.'

'Thanks.' Hilt was faintly surprised by Weston's change of heart. He went to the roan and checked his gear, tightening the cinch a little. Swinging into the saddle, he waited for the doctor to join him. Errol mounted a powerful chestnut and lifted a hand in farewell. Hilt rode in beside the doctor and they cantered across the yard and departed.

The night was dark but countless stars overhead gave enough light for them to ride easily. The trail was faint but Errol set a fast pace. Hilt maintained a close watch on the surrounding shadows, aware that the night could conceal bushwhackers itching to shoot anyone leaving Diamond O.

Time passed quickly, and when the distant lights of Cedar Creek showed in the distance, Errol slowed his pace and broke his silence.

'I don't envy you,' he observed. 'Soon as the towns-folk learn that you've throwed in with Diamond O you'll be up to your neck in trouble.'

'Why is that?' Hilt was interested. 'You said you've seen a lot in your travels around the county, Doc. Can you set me straight on a couple of points?'

'Name them.'

'Firstly, the Big D ranch. Is Hank Downey the one raising hell hereabouts?'

'Some things that have happened seem to point Downey' s way, but don't go along with first impressions. There's a lot of smoke on the range that is cloaking perception. Someone is playing a deep game, and all the cards aren't on the table yet. If you wanta find Billy Ormond when we ride in then go to the Black Ace Saloon. Chuck and Sue aren't aware of it yet, but Billy has got himself in with a bad bunch. He's drinking and gambling, but, hell, ain't that what a young man is supposed to do before he settles down? I sure don't blame him, but he should be more careful with things being as they are.'

'And the sheriff?' Hilt asked.

'You met him out at the ranch, huh? Yeah, he would give a man like you second thoughts.'

'A man like me?'

'No offence, Blaine, but I can read you. I don't approve of gunmen generally, but what you did at Diamond O proves that you have a moral back-ground. You can only be good for the Ormonds, and they sure will need some gun help before it's done. Now, Rafe Catlin is a killer, so don't let his cool manner throw you. I haven't worked out yet just what his game is, but he means to come out on top, however the cards fall. He's got rid of a lot of the bad men around here, but the trouble still continues, which to me means only one thing - Catlin has brought in his own men and they are looking after his interests. So don't trust the law.'

'You're aware of all this but done nothing about it?'

Errol chuckled harshly. 'You reckon I'm that big a fool, huh? Think about it. I'm no great shakes with a gun, and I'm always riding out alone. If I started wagging my chin and Catlin got to hear about it, how far do you think I'd get?'

'But you're telling me about it,' Hilt pursued.

'Sure. I've learned a great deal about human nature, son, and I got you pegged dead to rights. I reckon you're gonna set this range on fire, and all because of a gal named Sue Ormond. I saw you look at her back on the ranch, and you're hooked. Men are gonna die because you've taken a fancy to Sue.'

'I don't know where you got that from,' Hilt retorted. 'I don't see it like that. I would have stepped in if Sue Ormond was sixty years old and had a wooden leg. I can't stand by if a woman is being treated badly.'

'Sure,' Errol chuckled and urged his horse forward.

Hilt was thoughtful as they continued, and looked around with interest when they entered the main street. Cedar Creek seemed alive with buzzing movement. The sidewalks, illuminated by glaring lanterns, were thronged with men seemingly pleasure-bent, which surprised Hilt until he remembered that it was Saturday night. He reined in before the Black Ace saloon, with its garish lights and tinkling music. The batwings were in continual motion as men thronged inside. A gun crashed somewhere along the street and echoes drifted, but nothing disturbed the fast tenor of agitated life that seemed to be normal here.

'I did warn you about this,' Errol said, smiling grimly. 'And I can't join in. I've got to see a couple of patients. Good luck. I hope I don't have to see you in a professional capacity.'

'Thanks, Doc.' Hilt touched the brim of his Stetson with a long forefinger as Errol departed. 'See you around.'

He dismounted and wrapped his reins around the rail in front of the Black Ace. Pausing to take in his surroundings, he wished he had managed to arrive during daylight. But his main priority was to locate Billy Ormond and send him home. He mounted the steps to the sidewalk and pushed through the men standing around the entrance to the saloon. He was at least a head taller than most of them and they gave way reluctantly. Shouldering open the batwings, he stepped into the big, noisy room.

The blast of sound that struck Hilt as he crossed the threshold was like a physical force. Innumerable voices blotted out just about all else, including a player who was hammering relentlessly on an old upright piano in a corner. There was a long bar on the right, stretching the whole length of the room, and it was crowded with cowpokes in from the local ranches, some of them standing two and three deep. Four harassed tenders were busy supplying beer and liquor and trying to keep the bar top dry.

Gambling occupied the rest of the saloon. Small tables were busy with card players; there was every kind of games of chance, all busy with thronging pleasure-seekers intent on losing their cash. Saloon girls were circulating through the massed assembly, busy like flies feeding off a dead carcass.

Hilt stepped to one side of the batwings and looked around the room, seeking a glimpse of Billy Ormond. He spotted the youngster sitting at a corner table with four other men, and pushed through the crowd until he was standing just behind the youngster. He gauged the men at the table and decided that Billy was way out of his depth. This had to be the big game of the night, and he wondered why the others had let Billy, a comparative novice, play with them. His keen gaze soon discovered why. Billy was being cheated, and the youngster was becoming frustrated, although he could not see the steal. He was just a lamb that was ripe for fleecing.

'I never had such bad luck!' Billy threw in a losing hand. 'I can't do a blamed thing right. If I didn't know better, Hussey, I'd say this game is crooked.'

'You better smile when you say that or I might get the wrong idea. If you can't stand to lose then you shouldn't play with men. I'll give you a word of advice, Ormond: don't shoot off your big mouth unless you can back up your talk with powder smoke.' The big man uttering the threat was seated opposite Billy. Dressed in a dark-grey store suit, there was a long black cigar protruding at an angle from his thin slit of a mouth. He was sleek and soft-looking, but his tawny eyes were without humour, narrowed against the curling smoke that arose from his mouth. He regarded Billy for a moment, then smiled. 'You might be Old Man Ormond's son, but that don't cut no ice in here. So put up or shut up.'

'Don't give me that kinda hogwash!' Billy bridled instantly. 'You're the one running off at the lip, you damn four-flusher! Think I was born yesterday? No one could have such bad luck unless it was fixed.'

'Easy, Billy.' The man on the youngster's left, middle-aged and obviously one of the ranching fraternity, reached out and placed a placating hand on Billy's left arm. 'Easy does it, son. There's no need to get riled up. I ain't seen nothing going on that points to cheating. Why don't you settle up and get back to the Diamond O? You don't even know if your pa is gonna recover from his wound, and you're sitting here like it was an everyday event.

'I've a mind to quit,' Billy responded. 'But I don't like losing out to a tin-horn gambler.'

Hilt was aware that a hush had settled on the saloon. No glasses chinked; the piano player had frozen into immobility. A stillness pervaded the smoky atmosphere and taut faces were shining with sweat. Ben Hussey was motionless, a tight smile on his smooth face. He did not move a muscle, and Hilt, watching intently, considered that the gambler did not think the right moment for action had arrived.

'Why don't you quit yapping?' Hussey asked quietly. 'We'd like to get on with the game. If you think you're being gypped, Ormond, then drop out now and see me later, when I ain't busy. There's only one way to deal with your kind.'

'I ain't a quitter,' Billy rasped. 'Win or lose, I don't pull out that easy. You ain't gonna win nohow, Hussey. I'll play you to hell and back!'

'I'm getting a mite tired of your whining.' Hussey's manner changed instantly, his smooth exterior gone. His eyes had become hard and cold, and his right hand was resting on the gaming table, lined up on Billy.

Hilt tensed, certain that the gambler had a hideout gun in his right sleeve and was fixing to use it. He was aware that Billy had been set up, and knew the youngster had not a hope in hell of extricating himself without help. He waited for the expected eruption, and was ready when the action exploded.

FOUR

Billy Ormond cursed as he pushed back his chair and reached for the gun on his right hip. The men standing around the table watching the play ducked instinctively. Hilt saw Hussey flick his right hand and, as the muzzle of a .32 hideout gun slid into the gambler's grasp, drew his Colt and fired in a lightning-fast movement. The blasting shot racketed through the long room, shocking everyone. The bullet tore into Hussey's hand, smashing bones and boring flesh, then flattened against the small gun and ricocheted up into Hussey's shoulder.

Hussey screeched in agony and clasped his smashed fingers with his left hand, his wide eyes fixed in a shocked gaze at Hilt's grim figure and the deadly pistol now lined up on his chest. Blood was showing on his shirt where the ricochet had caught him. He slumped forward, his face hit the table, and he became inert.

Billy Ormond was frozen in a crouching position, his gun half drawn, his startled gaze on the man backing him. He recognized Hilt, and astonishment crept into his expression.

Everyone else in the room was motionless, staring at the corner table, and only Hilt's harsh voice, when it sounded, broke the bonds of shock that held them.

'It's time you went home, Billy.' Hilt spoke smoothly, his face showing no tension. 'Go on, get out of here.'

'What the hell!' the youngster rapped angrily. 'I don't need a nursemaid. What did you horn in for?'

'It was a set-up.' Hilt did not relax his vigilance and his gun continued to cover the men at the table. 'If I hadn't stepped in, you'd be dead now. Do like I say and get out of here.'

Ben Hussey stirred and pushed himself into a sitting position, his face pale. 'Who in hell are you, stranger?' he demanded unsteadily. Blood was dripping from his shattered hand. His eyes were filled with raw hatred as he gazed at Hilt.

'I'm on the Diamond O payroll to protect the Ormond family, and I know a set-up when I see one,' Hilt told him. 'And you were fixing to murder Billy. I'd sure like to know why before I kill you.'

'You're crazy!' Hussey became animated as his shock receded. 'What the hell! You'll pay for this, mister. No tin-horn gunnie can walk in here and shoot me!'

'I just did, and it's no big deal.' Hilt did not relax his alertness. His gun was cocked and ready for further action but nobody who had witnessed his draw was prepared to go against him. The big room was throbbing with tension, alive with a vibrant fear that tremored through the atmosphere.

'Was it a set-up, Hussey?' Billy demanded, his tone shaky. 'What was the game; plain murder, or an attempt to get at Diamond O through me?'

'You're crazy.' Hussey stifled a groan as he glanced around the crowded room. 'For God's sake, someone fetch the doctor,' he snarled.

'I'll kill the first man who moves,' Hilt rasped, and stillness followed his warning. He raised his voice, which echoed slightly in the silence as he continued, 'I got hired this afternoon because I stopped a couple of drygulchers who were trying to murder Chuck and Sue Ormond. Then the Diamond O was hit by a bunch of two-bit gunnies, and most of them died. So there's some kind of a war going on against the Ormonds, and I'm standing up for the family. If anyone has got something against the brand then call me out. I'm paying Ormond debts.'

He fell silent and waited, but there were no takers. When he looked around, men dropped their gaze. The card players at the table were still frozen in shock, and Hilt spoke to the man on Billy's left, who had tried to calm the youngster.

'What's your name?' he demanded.

'Will Spenser. I own Bar S north of Diamond O. I'm shocked by what you said. Me and Chuck Ormond go back a long way.'

'Have you been getting trouble?' Hilt demanded. 'Someone is out to steal Diamond O, and I'm wondering just how big the business is. Will the thieves be satisfied with the Ormond place or try for the whole range?'

'Nobody is going to run me off my place,' Spenser said. He was tall and thin, dressed in good range clothes, and there was a glitter in his dark eyes that told Hilt a great deal about him. 'If what you say is true then I can believe Billy was set up here.' He looked across the table at Hussey, who was hunching over again. 'What have you got to say, Hussey? Are you mixed up in this?'

'The hell I am!' Hussey stifled a groan. 'I'm a gambler. I make my money across this table. I ain't interested in beef or range.'

'But you set up Billy,' Spenser insisted. 'I saw it, but I didn't believe it at the time.'

There was a commotion at the batwings. Hilt heard the swing doors open and then close, and men began moving aside to reveal Sheriff Catlin and a tough-looking deputy coming forward. Both lawmen were carrying shotguns. Catlin paused across the table from Hilt, his features bland, but his eyes were calculating.

'I had a notion you might come into town and get caught up in local events.' Catlin smiled. 'Put up your gun, Blaine. I'll handle this. 'Toll, fetch the doctor before Hussey bleeds to death.' He waited for his deputy to move off, then nodded. 'Someone tell me what happened.'

Hilt holstered his gun and stood motionless. Several men began telling the sheriff what had occurred, and the law man lifted a hand and cut them off, impatience showing on his fleshy face. He directed his gaze at the men around the table, and his voice crackled when he spoke.

'Spenser, you're sitting here, and I don't reckon you're mixed up in anything going on, so tell me what happened.'

Hilt listened to the Bar S rancher's narrative, his right hand down at his side. He seemed to be completely at ease, but inside, he was like a coiled snake ready to strike. Catlin listened patiently to what Spenser had to say and, when the rancher lapsed into silence, he nodded.

'I've been watching points around town for a long time now,' he mused, 'and I don't like what I've seen. I've run out a lot of the hardcases, but I haven't got rid of the real troublemakers. I guess it's time I started in on them, and this business will lead me into a clean-up. Blaine, take Billy with you and get out of town. Go back to Diamond O and get ready for real trouble, because I reckon there's more coming your way.'

Hilt nodded without hesitation. 'On your way, Billy,' he said. 'You should be on the ranch taking care of your father and sister instead of trying to buck the weasels in here.'

Billy looked as if he wanted to argue about the decision but Catlin gave him no choice.

'Get out now, or spend the night in jail, Billy,' he rapped.

Billy drew a deep breath, sighed heavily, and walked around the table. His boots thudded on the sanded pine boards as he made for the batwings, and Hilt followed a couple of paces behind, glancing around at the watchful men who stepped aside for them. Billy thrust through the batwings and paused to hold them open for Hilt and, as he stood motionless in the lamplight, a gun blasted raucously from across the street, splitting the dense shadows with a long ribbon of reddish muzzle-flame.

Hilt lunged forward as Billy threw himself headlong across the sidewalk. Hitting the swinging batwings with his left shoulder, Hilt's gun was already in his hand. The pistol across the street fired again, and Hilt, in the act of going down into cover, paused on one knee and fired three swift shots at the gun flashes showing briefly opposite, bracketing the darkness.

He waited on one knee, gun uplifted, while the echoes of the shooting died away. There was no reply from across the street, but he continued to wait until the evening breeze had dissipated the gunsmoke around him.

'Do you reckon you got him?' Billy demanded, as an uneasy silence returned.

'Either that, or he's made a run for it.' Hilt's narrowed eyes continued probing the shadows around them.

'What in hell is going on out there?' Catlin yelled from inside the doorway of the saloon.'

Hilt listened to Billy's shouted reply, and got to his feet as the sheriff emerged from the saloon. Catlin stood erect in the lamplight, looking around, his gun holstered although he carried a shotgun, and Hilt again wondered about the lawman. Catlin was taking too much for granted, unless he knew more about the underlying situation than he admitted, and the doctor's assertion that Catlin was a killer lay heavily in Hilt's mind.

The sound of running footsteps along the sidewalk alerted the sheriff and he lifted his shotgun into the ready position as he faced the direction from which they were coming. The next instant his deputy arrived, breathing heavily, a pistol in his right hand cocked and ready for action, his shotgun gripped in his left hand.

'What in hell's goin' on, Rafe? What was the shooting?'

'Nothing to worry about, Toll,' Catlin replied. 'Just a spot of cleaning-up. Where's the doc?'

'He ain't at home so I left word for him to come on here when he can.'

Catlin nodded. 'Go into the saloon and stay with Hussey until Errol shows, then take Hussey to the law office. Charge him with disturbing the peace. I'll see you later. I've got some rooting around to do.'

The deputy nodded and went into the saloon. Catlin glanced at Hilt.

'Let's take a look across the street and see if you nailed that ambusher, huh?' He went to the nearest lantern, lifted it from a post, and started across the street.

Hilt followed closely, and heard Billy's movements as the youngster followed him. Catlin walked to an alley opposite and held the lantern high to cast light through the shadows. The alley was deserted, but the illuminating glare showed splotches of blood on the wall of the gunsmith's shop, where the gunman had been standing when Hilt opened fire. A sparse

63

trail of blood leading into the alley showed where the man had fled.

'That looks promising,' Catlin observed. 'Let's see how far he got. I'll bet he didn't reach the back lots.'

They walked along the alley, and Hilt dropped back a couple of yards from the sheriff in order to see better. Black shadows enshrouded them as they proceeded, and they reached the back lots without sighting their quarry. Catlin moved out from the alley, the lantern held high, and Hilt caught a glimpse of a saddle horse standing nearby, with a motionless figure lying huddled on its face almost beside the animal. The horse whickered nervously as they approached.

'Blaine, I could do with you as a deputy,' Catlin observed, as he bent over the figure. 'That was mighty nice shooting.'

'I already got a job,' Hilt replied, 'and I reckon it'll be as much as I can handle before it's done.'

Catlin laughed. He grasped the shoulder of the fallen man and pulled him over on to his back. Billy Ormond uttered a cry of shock and came pushing to Hilt's side.

'That's Floyd Meeker!' he said in amazement.

'His name means nothing to me,' Hilt rasped.

'He's on our payroll! One of our cowhands.'

'Not any more, he ain't,' Catlin said callously. 'He's cashed his chips.' He looked up at Hilt. 'I wonder who he was trying to nail, you or Billy?'

'Billy left the saloon ahead of me,' Hilt mused. 'The first shot was fired before I stepped out. So he was after Billy.'

'Why would Floyd wanta shoot me?' Billy

demanded in a distressed tone. 'We were good friends. We came into town together many times. He ain't but a couple of years older'n me.'

'If we knew his motive we might get the answers to a lot of questions that need to be asked,' Catlin observed.

'Was he on the ranch when the shooting took place this afternoon?' Hilt asked.

'He was,' Catlin nodded. 'I saw him there.'

'I wonder if he traded lead with the raiders?' Hilt shook his head. 'Billy, we better be getting back to the ranch. Where's your horse?'

'In the livery barn. I'll go and get it.'

'We'll go together,' Hilt retorted. 'We don't take any chances until we know what's going on. ' He glanced at the watchful sheriff. 'Do you need me for anything before I ride out?'

'Nope. I'll know where to find you if I do need you. I guess I don't have to tell you to keep the Ormond family close to the ranch until we've sorted this out, huh?'

'You can count on me,' Hilt replied.

They went back to the street and Hilt collected the roan from the front of the saloon, where a dozen or so men were standing on the boardwalk, waiting to learn the details of the shooting. No one spoke to Hilt, but there was a clamour of voices when the sheriff went in among them.

Hilt walked along the street with Billy siding him, heading for the livery barn. Billy was badly shocked by the knowledge that Floyd Meeker had tried to shoot him.

'I can't believe it,' he said. ' Floyd shot at me the minute I stepped out of the saloon. He must have known it was me.'

'We won't learn from him why he did it,' Hilt replied, 'but we might be able to piece things together when we get back to Diamond O. I want to know why Meeker was in town.' He paused, and added as an afterthought, 'Did you know that a bunch of riders came to the ranch after you left to fetch Doc Errol?'

'No. You said something about it in the saloon, and I wondered what you meant. What happened?'

Hilt narrated the grim facts, and Billy was silent for some moments before drawing a deep breath and sighing heavily.

'I owe you a big vote of thanks,' he said contritely. 'If you hadn't stepped in when you saw Pa and Sue being shot at they would surely have been killed. And then the raid on the ranch. And you saved me back there in the saloon. Hussey would have killed me if you hadn't showed up.'

'And there were the two men I found at the Big D line shack. I guess their actions tie in Big D to the trouble.'

'We'll have to take the outfit over to Big D and have a showdown with Hank Downey,' Billy said grimly. 'It's the only way to settle this business. If we sit back and let them have it all their own way they'll pick us off.'

They reached the livery barn. There was a lantern burning over the big wide-open doorway, where an old man was standing at ease, leaning on a pitchfork.

'Say, you've got Art Weston's roan,' Billy observed.

'He lent it to me. My buckskin had run itself out.'

'Art lent you his favourite horse?' Billy shook his head. 'You must be something else, Blaine. Weston wouldn't let his own mother ride that horse.'

'I had some trouble from him when I rode into the ranch,' Hilt admitted. 'But he sure mellowed after the raid and I fetched in those two prisoners. Get your bronc, Billy, and let's mosey out of here. I'd like to come back in daylight and take a look around. But I got a feeling there could be more trouble at the ranch before sun-up. Let's split the breeze.'

'What was all the shooting about?' the liveryman asked Hilt, when Billy had gone into the barn.

Hilt explained some of it and the oldster shook his head.

'I don't know what this town is coming to,' he said sadly. 'It wasn't this troublesome back in the old days. There's a bad bunch gathering in the county, and that can mean only one thing: the vultures are preparing to pick over someone's bones, or my name ain't John Ketchum.'

'Do you now who's behind it?' Hilt asked.

Ketchum shook his head. 'All I know about is horses. And if I did know anything I'd keep my mouth shut.'

Billy emerged from the barn leading his horse, and they mounted and rode back along the street. Hilt held his reins in his left hand, the fingers of his right hand resting lightly on the butt of his holstered gun. The street was still busy, and as they passed the saloon a fist fight involving at least six men erupted on the sidewalk in front of the batwings.

'Never used to be this much trouble around here,' Billy commented. 'The town is all worked up over something. I never noticed it before, but it sure shows now.'

Hilt glanced over his shoulder at the brawling men, and saw two riders turning their mounts away from the tie rail in front of the saloon to come along the street at a canter.

'We could have company, Billy,' he said. 'Don't turn around, but there are two riders eating our dust. When we get out of town we'll push on fast and see if they're following us. If they are, we'll get the drop on them and find out what they're up to.'

'It'll be a pleasure,' Billy replied.

Hilt nodded and touched spurs to his mount, sending the animal out of the street at a canter. Billy sided him, and they left town fast, galloping through the darkness enveloping the trail. Hilt held their speed for 200 yards, then pulled his mount down to a walk.

'Keep riding for another hundred yards,' he instructed the youngster, 'then halt and wait. I'll pull off the trail here and get behind those two. Whatever happens, don't start shooting. You might hit me. Just be ready to duck any lead that might come your way.'

'Sure thing.' Billy spurred his mount again and went on.

As the sound of hoofs faded, Hilt rode off the trail and turned to face the now distant town. Within moments he heard the pounding of hoofs coming towards him, and then two riders galloped by, leaving a banner of dust hanging in the night. Hilt urged his horse back on to the trail and picked up speed. He badly needed to know who was plotting against Diamond O, and this was the only way he could find out.

FIVE

With the strong night breeze in his face, Hilt canted his head to one side and picked up the sound of the horses he had swung in behind. He could see the dim figures of the two riders who had passed him, and drew his pistol and cocked it. The men ahead were suddenly slowing, and Hilt cursed silently when Billy's voice suddenly rang through the night.

'Pull up there,' the youngster shouted. 'I'm Billy Ormond. Who's following me?'

A gun crashed immediately, the flash illuminating the two riders briefly in silhouette as one of them fired. Then a burst of gunfire shattered the night as both unknowns cut loose. Hilt lifted his gun and triggered the weapon. His first shot struck the right-hand man and sent him pitching out of his saddle. The second man reined in sharply and swung his mount to the left. A gun flash spurted from ahead of the man and Hilt knew that Billy had bought into the action. He fired at the disappearing rider and saw the indistinct figure fall from its saddle.

Hilt pulled his horse down to a walk as the echoes died slowly. He was breathing shallowly through his mouth. Silence closed in. The darkness was intense. He suddenly felt completely alone in an alien world, but shook off the eerie feeling of remoteness that swirled through him.

'Billy, where are you?' he called, and anger filtered through him because he had wanted to question the two unknowns. He needed to learn something of the background to the trouble that was breaking out on this range, and would have got the drop on the men and made them talk. He suppressed a sigh. 'Show yourself, Billy,' he rapped.

'Over here,' came the reply. 'We did good, huh? They started shooting at me the minute they heard my name. That proves it's the Ormonds they're after.'

'Yeah, but that wasn't what I told you to do.'

'We needed to know if they were after us, or were just a couple of riders going back to their ranch.' Billy was unrepentant. 'Keep me covered while I take a look at them. I'll know them by sight, if they work around here.'

'Be careful. They might still be alive, and they're armed.' Hilt remained on edge while Billy dismounted and went to the first of the two men.'

'This one is dead,' the youngster announced. 'I'll need to strike a match to identify him.'

'Check the other one first,' Hilt rapped. 'If he's still breathing, you'll give him a good shot at you.'

'Yeah.' Billy turned and came along the trail to where a horse was standing beside its fallen rider.

Dropping to one knee, he checked the figure. 'This one is dead as well,' he said. 'Hold on and I'll get a light on him.'

Hilt dismounted and trailed his reins. He walked forward until he stood looking down at the motionless figure. A match scraped and a tiny pinpoint of light dispelled the immediate gloom. Billy uttered a gasp as he shielded the flame and got a look at the dead, upturned face.

'Jeez!' he gasped. 'It's Jed Toll, dead as a nail.'

'Who's Toll?' Hilt demanded.

Billy stood up and the match was extinguished. 'He's the chief deputy sheriff, that's all.'

Hilt was shocked. His teeth clicked together. 'Toll was the deputy who came into saloon with the sheriff, huh?'

'That's right. ' Billy turned back to the other man and bent over the corpse, striking another match to check the stiffening features. 'This is Steve Yelding,' he announced, and came back to confront Hilt, his face a pale blur in the faint starlight. 'What are we gonna do, Blaine? This couldn't be worse. Yelding is a deputy, too. I think we're in bad trouble. There'll be hell to pay when Catlin gets word of this.'

'You challenged them,' Hilt mused. 'Did you fire the first shot?'

'The hell I did! They started shooting soon as I opened my mouth. Heck, that first shot scorched my face. If you hadn't been so fast in replying, they would have got me for sure.'

'And they followed us out of town,' Hilt nodded. 'They saw us leaving and came after us, then started shooting without warning. So what does that make them? And did they follow us on the sheriff's orders? If they did then we are in big trouble. Or were they in cahoots with the man back of the trouble? Heck, they must be after big stakes, coming out into the open like that.'

'You're thinking deep,' Billy complained. 'Them's mighty powerful questions you're coming up with.'

'And I need answers to them.' Hilt drew a deep breath. 'Billy, go on back to the ranch like this never happened, I'll take these two back to town and see what Catlin's got to say about this.'

'You can't do that!' Billy was aghast at Hilt's audacity. 'Hell, Catlin will gun you down or toss you in jail.'

'I don't think so. But someone is out to get you planted. It was tried in the saloon, and then these two came to finish the job. So go back to Diamond O and stay there. If Catlin comes out there, tell him we left town together and I dropped back because someone was following us. You heard shooting but kept riding so you don't know what happened. That'll put you in the clear, and I'll take my chances with Catlin.'

'That don't hardly seem right,' Billy said doubtfully.

'It's about time you started doing as you're told,' Hilt retorted. 'This isn't a game. Someone is out to steal Diamond O, and they don't care much how they do it. You get on back to the ranch and stay there. I need to learn a thing or two before I can leave here, so make my job easier by doing like I tell you.'

'I'll go along with that,' Billy sighed, reluctance sounding in his voice, but he turned instantly and went to his horse. Swinging into the saddle, he sat for a moment, looking at Hilt's grim figure. 'I sure hope you know what you're doing. Catlin is hell on wheels when he gets going.'

'So long,' Hilt replied, and stood motionless while Billy rode away. He waited until the sound of the youngster's hoofs faded, then loaded the two bodies on to their horses and tied the animals together. Mounting the roan, he headed back to Cedar Creek, leading the burdened animals, and his thoughts turned ceaselessly as he mulled over what had happened.

He was still uncertain of his actions when he reached the outskirts of Cedar Creek. What he really wanted to know was where the sheriff stood in this business, and he didn't think he would learn much if he rode in boldly with the bodies and reported what had happened. He turned aside from the trail and rode into a thicket, where he tied the horses and dumped the two bodies in the long grass, intending to return for them later.

When he rode on he was prepared for trouble in any guise. He eased his gun in its holster and entered the wide street, moving at a walking pace. The sound of the roan's hoofs was muffled in the thick dust. Entering an alley on the right, he traversed it to the back lots and tethered the roan in cover, then walked back to the street, pausing to locate the sheriff's office.

The law building was standing alone on the left-hand side of the street with an alley on either side. The Cattleman's Bank was its neighbour on the nearer side and a general store stood on the far side. A lantern was burning dimly on an awning post to the right of the office door. Hilt spotted a figure standing in the shadows on the sidewalk in front of the office and moved in slowly, keeping to the dense shadows. He saw the glow of a lighted cigarette as the unknown man smoked intermittently.

Hilt gained the alley beside the law office and stood motionless in its cover. The man on the sidewalk was barely a dozen feet away and, despite his efforts, Hilt could not get a clear look at him. He fancied it was Catlin, but the nearby lantern was too dim to permit definite identification.

Minutes passed and Hilt waited patiently. He could hear music, muted by distance, and reviewed what had happened in the saloon. Billy Ormond had been set up, and would have been killed but for Hilt's intervention. The figure on the sidewalk suddenly began to pace up and down, as if his patience was running out, and when he passed the lantern and turned to retrace his steps, his features became visible to Hilt's keen gaze. He nodded slowly. It was Rafe Catlin.

Some minutes later, footsteps sounded on the boardwalk and Hilt, peering around the front corner of the building, saw two men coming towards the sheriff. Catlin paused and turned to face them. The newcomers, both dressed in travel-stained range clothes, were wearing gunbelts, and they halted before Catlin.

'You sure took your time getting here, Poggin,' Catlin observed. 'This business has been hotting up, and then some. I could have done with you this afternoon. All hell has busted loose. I told you I needed your help urgently, so what in hell kept you?'

'A little necessary business,' Poggin replied, his teeth glinting when he smiled. He was tall and broad, with a swagger about him that pointed to his temperament. 'This is my sidekick, Jack Kemble. We're here now, so cut the cackle. What do you want done, Rafe?'

'There's a gunnie showed up around here name of Frank Blaine. I don't think that's his right name. I checked my dodgers but he ain't among them. But I've got a bad feeling about him. He's gone in with the Ormonds, and could blow this deal apart. He stepped in this afternoon when Chuck Ormond was due to be killed, and stopped Jenson and Leat in their tracks. He's hell on wheels, and I need him put out of it.'

'It'll cost you five hundred bucks,' Poggin responded.

'Half now and the rest when he's dead,' Catlin growled. 'Come into the office and I'll pay you. When he's gone there'll be a few more jobs you can handle for me. I can't afford to waste any more time. The pot has been boiling too long as it is.'

Catlin turned and led the way into the office and the two men followed. Hilt saw the men's features as they entered the office. The one called Poggin was bearded, with a hawk-like nose and a thin trap of a mouth. The other was of medium build, fleshy, and wearing a bushy moustache. He looked around carefully as he entered the office, his keen eyes flitting across the blackness of the alley mouth where Hilt was concealed, indicating a cautious nature.

Hilt moved to a window in the alley and peered into the law office. He saw Catlin produce a wad of notes, count off some, and give them to Poggin. Catlin was speaking seriously, his voice inaudible now, but Hilt had heard enough to set him straight on the sheriff. Catlin had just paid these two men to kill him.

He stood thinking about the development. So Doc Errol was right in his judgement that Catlin was a killer. But knowing the fact was one thing and doing something about it was another. And now there were two tough-looking killers on his tail. Hilt smiled mirthlessly. He was holding a slight advantage at the moment, but needed to act immediately to maintain it.

Catlin talked for some time to the newcomers, then sat down behind his desk and busied himself with paperwork. Poggin and Kemble left the office and went back along the sidewalk towards the saloon. Hilt followed them, staying back in the shadows. When they entered the Black Ace, he waited outside, watching them through a window. They bellied up to the long bar and stood drinking as if they had all the time in the world. But Hilt was familiar with their kind, and knew they would not waste much time before attempting to carry out Catlin's wishes.

After twenty minutes, Kemble emerged from the

saloon. Hilt followed the gunman to the stable and watched from the shadows while two horses were saddled. Before Kemble could lead the animals out, Hilt entered the stable and approached him. Drawing his gun, he cocked it, and the ominous sound alerted the man. Kemble swung around, reaching for his holstered gun as he did so, but froze when he saw Hilt and the gun that was levelled at his chest.

'What's this, a hold-up?' Kemble demanded. 'You picked the wrong man, mister. I ain't got a dime.'

'It's you I want,' Hilt replied. 'Catlin has paid Poggin to kill Frank Blaine.'

Kemble gazed at him impassively, then asked, 'Who are you?'

'Frank Blaine.' Hilt returned his gun to its holster and dropped his hand to his side. 'You get first shot at me,' he said. 'I'll look up Poggin after this.'

'Now wait a minute. That deal was between Poggin and Catlin. It ain't got nothing to do with me.'

'That's too bad. You can make your play any time. If you beat me, ask Poggin for the money.'

'I ain't drawing against you,' Kemble shook his head and lifted his hands shoulder high. 'Go face Poggin.'

'If that's the way you want it.' Hilt began to turn away as if intent on leaving, but he was watching Kemble closely.

The instant Kemble was out of a direct line of fire he dropped his hands and made a play for his gun. Hilt swung back to face him, unmoving until Kemble had actually started to draw his weapon.

The instant Kemble's gun cleared leather, Hilt moved. His hand flashed to the butt of his gun and came up levelling the weapon with the speed of a striking snake. He thumbed back the hammer before the pistol was levelled, and the weapon exploded with a crashing detonation.

Kemble was in the act of cocking his gun when Hilt's bullet took him to the right of centre in the chest. The impact of the shot hurled him back against his horse and the gun flew from his hand as he fell to the ground. Hilt restrained his breathing as gunsmoke filled his nostrils. He turned and left the stable quickly, moving to a wagon that was standing in the stable yard.

He could see the street from his position and expected someone to come and check on the shooting. But minutes passed and no one showed. He shook his head. His ears were ringing faintly from the crash of his shot. The cool night breeze blowing in from the range was strangely cold against his face. He remained motionless.

When he heard a faint movement somewhere in the shadows to his right he dropped a hand to the butt of his gun but did not draw the weapon. Moments passed, and then he saw a slight movement of the shadows some yards away. He narrowed his eyes in an attempt to catch a glimpse of the newcomer, but nothing showed in the impenetrable darkness. He crouched a little.

Time was of no importance in the stalking business, and Hilt waited patiently for developments. When he heard another slight sound he smiled to himself, turning his head slowly as he tried to pinpoint it. Then he caught the louder sound of boots thudding on the sidewalk along the street and his smile faded.

A man suddenly appeared out of the shadows, walking boldly towards the stable door. Hilt watched his progress, unable to see more than a dim outline. The man passed the spot where Hilt thought the stalker was standing, and there was a sullen thud followed by a low cry of pain, then the sound of a body hitting the ground.

Silence returned, and Hilt waited. Presently he saw a movement by the doorway of the stable, and then a figure eased out of the surrounding darkness and passed through the faintly lit doorway like a wraith, gun in hand and intent on getting into cover beyond the light.

Hilt moved away from the wagon and sought the left-hand corner of the barn, his gaze unblinking as he kept the doorway of the building under observation. He had failed to identify the moving figure and wanted to see more. Walking slowly towards the open doorway, gun in hand, he paused at a knot-hole in the sun-bleached boards and looked through it.

The newcomer was bending over Kemble, holding a pistol in his right hand, and he was a stranger to Hilt, who had half-expected to see Poggin. But this was a much older man and of a different size. He saw the man search Kemble, removing some articles which he put into his own pockets.

When the man came back to the doorway, Hilt was waiting outside, gun ready, and struck for the man's gun wrist with the barrel of his .45. The man cursed in pain as his weapon fell from a suddenly nerveless hand.

'Freeze,' Hilt told him, pressing his muzzle against the side of the man's neck. 'You've just robbed a dead man. Who are you?'

'Don't shoot,' the man gasped. 'I'm Bill Varney. I heard a shot and came for a look-see. The dead man in there is a stranger. Did you kill him?'

'You've got a long nose, which ain't healthy. Are you a lawman?'

'Heck, no! Folks around here call me the town drunk, but I don't reckon I drink more than anyone else.'

'You're dangerous,' Hilt said. 'You hit the man coming to the stable.'

'That was Doc Errol. I wanted to check out the body before anyone else got to it. I don't cotton to the doc. He does some strange things for a medical man.'

'What do you do around town? In my experience, a drunk doesn't hold down a regular job.'

'You're right. I do odd jobs. Folks around here don't trust me none. I used to work in the bank, but that crook Blanchard, the banker, fired me for getting his books in a mess. But that was just his excuse. He wanted me out of it because I knew too much.'

'Too much about what?'

'The cause of the trouble building up around here.'

'Do you know what it is about?'

'That's why I was fired.'

'What turned you to drink?'

'My wife was killed two years ago. She got caught up in the crossfire that killed old Sheriff Benton. They said my wife's death was an accident, but I know it was murder. They killed her to get at me. If you're working for them and you're gonna kill me, mister, then get it done. You'll be doing me a favour, anyway.'

'You got a place where you bed down?' Hilt demanded.

'Yeah. A shack behind the Black Ace saloon. Ike Carmel, the saloonman, lets me use it. I do lots of jobs for Carmel.'

'Let's go there. I need to talk to you.' Hilt grasped the man's right arm and tugged him around so that lamplight fell upon him. He saw an oldish face that looked older than it really was, marked by dissolution and grief, unshaven and unwashed.

'There ain't nothing I could tell you,' Varney said. 'I don't interest myself in local affairs these days.'

'You must hear lots of talk, mooching around town, and folks tend to ignore a drunk. What did you get off Kemble?'

'A watch, and that's about all. What's it to you?'

'I'll pay you for any information you can give me. Real money. Does that interest you?'

'Money? Sure thing. Give me a couple of bucks, tell me what you wanta know, and I'm your man.'

'Then let's get out of here.' Hilt glanced around. He moved back to the left-hand corner of the barn, taking Varney with him, and as they passed around the corner into the darkness, he heard Doc Errol groaning as he recovered his senses.

Retaining his hold on Varney, Hilt instructed the man to lead him to his shack. The night was dark, with little starshine to relieve the gloom, and Varney stumbled around a lot as they progressed across the back lots. Hilt, with a good sense of direction, soon felt that they were wandering off-line, and shook Varney with considerable force.

'We're making for your shack, remember,' he snapped. 'If you're trying to fool me then forget it.'

'I ain't fooling anybody. I just don't remember so well any more. Must be the drink. Too much whiskey ain't good for the memory. Where are we now? I don't see too well in the dark.'

'We're on the back lots, heading towards the Black Ace. You said your shack is behind the saloon, didn't you?'

'Yeah. That's right. Can't be far now.'

Hilt kept moving, taking Varney with him, and they came eventually to a ramshackle little building with an ill-fitting door and a roof which was missing several shingles and seemed to lean at a dangerous angle.

'This the place?' Hilt demanded.

'That's it. I got a key somewhere. Have to keep it locked. There are a lot of thieves in town these days.'

'Let's get inside then.' Hilt was having doubts about the wisdom of trying to get information from a drunk, but he needed to know the background to the local situation. He waited while Varney tried unsuccessfully to unlock the door, then took the key from the man and did it for him.

'You got a match?' Varney demanded. 'I'm fresh out.'

Hilt produced a match and struck it, squinting as dim light flared. He saw a lantern standing on a small table and lit it, then looked around. Home to Varney was primitive and dirty. Apart from the table and a chair, there was a bunk in a corner and little else. The place stank like a pigsty. Hilt closed the door and regarded Varney, who slumped on the chair and returned Hilt's gaze with dull eyes that seemed strangely unfocused.

'What do you wanta know, mister?' Varney demanded. He reached for an empty whiskey bottle standing on the table. 'Ah, I need a drink.' His hands shook as he withdrew the cork from the bottle and lifted it to his slack lips, sucking greedily.

Hilt shook his head, thinking that Varney was too far gone to be of any help. But he restrained his impatience, needing information, and prepared to draw out his unsteady companion.

SIX

Hilt produced a handful of coins and threw two dollars on to the table in front of Varney, who grabbed up the money and thrust it into a pocket.

'So, what do you wanta know?' Varney demanded.

'Tell me why you were fired from the bank?'

'Because I knew too much.' Varney shook his head.

'Knew too much about what?'

'The crooked deal that half the businessmen in town have got their fingers in.'

'Give me some details.'

'What's it to you? I ain't set eyes on you before. You're a stranger. There are too many of your kind around here.'

'I'm troubleshooting for Diamond O. I reckon the combine making trouble for the Ormonds is the one you had trouble with, so that kind of puts us on the same side, huh?'

'Maybe.' Varney passed a hand wearily across his eyes. 'God, I need a drink. You got any likker?'

'You can buy all you want after you've talked to

me. Keep your mind on what you're saying. What did you find out at the bank that got you fired?'

'Tom Blanchard, the banker, paid a couple of gunnies to shoot old Sheriff Benton so Catlin could wear the star. I overheard the arrangements. Catlin was the deputy here then, but it was the first law job he ever had. Before he came here he was a rustler along the Pecos. I heard him bragging about it to Blanchard. They got tied in with Hank Downey, who owns the Big D, and they reckon to clean out this range, lock, stock and barrel.' Varney slumped back in his seat and gazed blearily at Hilt. 'Anything else you wanta know?'

'Have you told anyone else about this? I'm wondering why they haven't killed you to shut your mouth.'

'They killed my wife to do that. I ain't gonna spill the beans to anyone, unless they pay me for it.'

'Who else is in on this crooked deal?'

'Who have I told you about?' Varney's eyes closed and he began to breathe heavily.

Hilt grasped the man's shoulder and shook his awake. 'Don't go to sleep on me,' he said crisply. 'Give me more names. You told me about Catlin, Blanchard, and Downey of Big D. Who else do you know about?'

'I learned nothing after I was fired, and that was a long time ago. But you can bet they've brought in other men to help them. Hell, ain't you got enough to be going on with? How much do you want for a coupla dollars?'

'Yeah, I guess you're right. Thanks. But I reckon you'd be pleased if those fellers were made to pay for what they did.' Hilt went to the door but paused when Varney spoke again.

'Be careful when you leave, mister.'

'Why?'

'Catlin don't trust me none. He's always got one of his badge toters watching me. If they've seen us come in here together then you could be in a lot of trouble. Mind they ain't waiting for you outside.'

Hilt nodded. 'Thanks for the warning.' He looked around the shack, saw a back door, and moved to it. 'I'll play safe and leave this way. See you around, Varney.'

He reached out to lift the wooden bar on the back door, and at that moment the front door was thrust open and a man appeared in the aperture. Hilt saw lanternlight glinting on a gun in the man's hand and dived to his left, drawing his gun as he did so. At the same instant a heavy hand shook the back door, and Catlin's voice rang out.

'We got you dead to rights, Varney. Don't give us no trouble, or you're dead. Come on out or we'll come in shooting.'

Hilt ducked, for the man standing in the front door began triggering his pistol. Bullets crackled across the small room. Hilt returned fire instantly, aiming past the motionless Varney, and his first slug smacked into the chest of the man in the doorway. He sprang up and went forward at a run, jumping over the falling body and leaving the shack fast.

Catlin started shooting through the back door but Hilt was in the clear and sprinting fast through the darkness. He reached the back of the Black Ace and paused in its shadow, breathing hard. Looking back at the shack, he saw a figure that looked like Catlin going in through the front door. Hilt turned and ran along the back of the saloon and then down the alley on the far side of the building.

He reached the street and paused to get his bearings. No one seemed to have heard the shooting, or they were uninterested. He crossed the street, making for the spot where he had tethered the roan. The animal whickered as he closed in on it and he paused to check out the surroundings. He made a wide circle around the animal, expecting to find someone staked out and waiting for him to show up, but there was no one.

Minutes later, he was riding away from Cedar Creek along the trail that led to Diamond O. His thoughts were buzzing with what he had learned from Varney. But had the man told the truth? He was inclined to believe every word of it, although he would make a check of his own. So now he knew enough about the situation to start operating. The banker, the sheriff and the Big D rancher were in cahoots in some kind of crooked business.

He grinned tensely as the roan hammered along the open trail towards Diamond O. There would be hell to pay in town when those two deputies were found, and now Hilt could understood why Catlin had ordered them out to commit murder.

He slowed the roan to an easier pace and they covered the distance to the ranch in quick time. When the lights of the house showed ahead, he pulled the horse down to a canter, and moments later a guarded challenge reached him from the shadows around the gate. Giving his name, he rode in close and dismounted to talk to the guard.

'Is Billy here?' he asked, as the guard opened the gate.

'Ain't seen hide nor hair of him since he rode out for the sawbones this afternoon,' the guard replied. 'Didn't you find him in town?'

Hilt rode on to the house, alarmed by the news and blaming himself for not staying with the youngster. He reined in at the porch and stepped down from the saddle. Art Weston was on the porch, sitting in deep shadow, and the foreman came forward to reveal himself.

'Thanks for the loan of the horse,' Hilt said. 'I never rode a better bronc.'

'Where's Billy?' Weston came off the porch and loosened the cinch on the roan. 'Didn't you see him in town?'

'I did better than that.' Hilt explained what had taken place, then added, 'Then I did a fool thing. I told Billy to come home alone while I looked around.'

'And he ain't showed.' Lamplight coming from a window shone on Weston's craggy face. He looked incredibly old. Hilt heard him sigh heavily. 'I'll get a search party out at first light,' Weston said. 'I expect he'll be somewhere along the trail.'

89

'You'd better come into the house and hear what I've got to say to the boss,' Hilt told him. 'If what I've learned is true then we can hogtie this business tomorrow.'

'What's happened?' Sue appeared in the doorway in time to hear Hilt's last words. 'I'm glad you're back, Blaine.'

'How is your father?' Hilt countered. 'Is he well enough to hear what I have to tell? I wouldn't want to have to run through it more than once.'

'Dad won't go to sleep until he knows that Billy is safe,' she responded. 'Did you see him in town?'

Hilt swallowed his impatience and crossed the porch to the door, and Sue fell back before him until she was standing inside the house. Weston followed noisily. Sue looked at Hilt's set features, decided that she did not like what she saw, and turned silently to lead the way up the stairs.

Chuck Ormond was awake, propped up in bed. His face was haggard, showing shock. He looked at Hilt as if he feared bad news. Hilt wasted no time in explaining what had happened in Cedar Creek from the moment he stepped into the Black Ace saloon until he gunned down the two deputies on the trail. Then he lapsed into silence to give them the opportunity to absorb his words.

'Does any of that make sense to you?' he asked.

Chuck Ormond shook his head. 'I don't know what to make of it,' he admitted. 'Why all this trouble now?'

Hilt glanced at the silent Weston. 'What about you?' he asked.

Weston shook his head. 'I never could make head or tail of what was going on around here,' he answered.

Hilt sighed. 'Well there's more to come, and maybe I can shed a little light on what's been happening.'

He related the rest of it; how he went back to town and eavesdropped on Catlin and then killed Kemble in the stable. When he mentioned Bill Varney coming on the scene and what ensued, Ormond stiffened in the bed, his fingers gripping the sheet. Weston cleared his throat a couple of times but said nothing. Having brought them up to date, Hilt lapsed into silence. Sue leaned forward, her face showing the nature of her thoughts.

'I always felt that Catlin was bad,' she mused. 'But is Varney to be believed? He's been the town drunk for years, and I would think his mind has been affected by his addiction.'

'I left him with Catlin going into the shack with a gun in his hand,' Hilt said, 'so perhaps Varney is dead now. I couldn't wait to find out. I needed to get back here and give you the facts, and tomorrow we'll start checking them out. We don't have to take anything at face value. And what about Big D?' He looked at Weston. 'Did you get anything more out of Cottrill and Pilk?'

'They won't talk.' Weston shook his head. 'How are we gonna get at the truth?'

'There are a couple of things I want to try tomorrow,' Hilt mused. 'I need to follow the tracks of those gunnies who came in here shooting. They'll lead right back to where those men started out, and if that is Big D then it'll be all the proof we'll need. I'll ride out at sun-up.'

'And the rest of us can sit around twiddling our thumbs until you get back, huh?' Weston demanded.

'Have you got a problem with that?' Hilt frowned. 'I'm gonna stick my neck out, and I don't need any of your men around to get in my way. Let me get the proof we need and then you'll be up to your eyes in the clean-up. There's no other way to play this, so hold your cards close to your vest and sit it out.'

'He's right,' Ormond said harshly. 'What's got into you, Art? This man has put his life on the line for us. Anyway, you've got a chore to handle tomorrow, and I want every man you can spare out on it.'

'Billy?' Sue demanded.

'Right.' Ormond nodded. 'I want him found, but fast. If you don't find his body then look for his tracks, and find him.'

Weston nodded grimly and turned to the door. 'We'll be in the saddle at daybreak,' he said heavily.

Hilt waited until the sound of the foreman's feet on the stairs faded away. He stifled a yawn. Sue was regarding him with narrowed eyes, evidently sifting through the information he had revealed.

'What about Poggin, the man Catlin paid to kill you?' she queried. 'He'll likely be holed up on the range watching the house come the dawn, waiting for you to show.'

'I expect so.' Hilt nodded. 'That's how I would handle it if I were in his boots, and that's why I'll be gone before the sun shows. I ain't worried about Poggin. He can wait. I need to find out where those raiders came from. I followed them a long way yesterday, and they looked like they were heading for Big D. But I need to know for sure. It's a pity Pilk didn't talk. Mebbe I ought to have a word with him. He might just open up to me. Where's Weston holding him and Cottrill?'

'In the bunkhouse.' Sue turned to the door. 'I must turn in,' she added, 'although I don't suppose I shall sleep. But my head is aching and my mind is buzzing. You'd better try and get some sleep, Dad.'

'That's right.' Hilt followed her as she left the room. 'I'll be gone early, but make sure nobody steps out of line around here before I get back.'

'How do you mean?' Her eyes looked tired as she studied his face.

'Don't let Weston go off half-cocked about anything. Make sure you got enough men on the spread at all times to defend it. There's no telling when you'll get another visit from those raiders.'

'You think they'll return?' Her face clouded. 'But you killed most of them.'

'Sure. But there'll be others, and next time they won't be taken by surprise. I'd like to be in two places at once tomorrow. But I need to get some proof so I've got to ride out. Don't even show yourself on the porch, huh? It's that dangerous.'

She nodded. 'How shall I ever be able to thank you for what you're doing?' she asked.

'I don't need thanks.' He shook his head,

descended the stairs, and went out to the porch.

The night was silent and still and that worried him. There was a thin crescent moon hanging in the dark overhead to the east and he looked around, listening intently. But with two guards out he did not think anyone could sneak in unseen. Seeing lights in the bunkhouse, he walked across the yard, and Weston challenged him from the shadows around the corral.

'It's Blaine,' he replied, and the foreman appeared at his side. 'I want to talk to Pilk. Is he in the bunkhouse?'

'Yeah. But he's a mean *hombre* and ain't willing to talk.'

'He might open up to me.' Hilt entered the bunkhouse, wrinkling his nose at the fetid smell emanating from the dozen or so punchers snoring in their bunks. A man was seated on a chair at the far end of the long building, a rifle in his hands, and he stood up as Hilt and Weston approached.

'Where's Pilk?' Weston demanded.

'Asleep there.' The guard pointed to the end bunk.

Hilt crossed to the man and shook him awake. Pilk groaned as he opened his eyes, and groaned again when he recognized Hilt.

'Ain't you the lucky one?' Hilt greeted. 'Flat out and pounding your ear while I'm still working. You could save everyone a lot of trouble and effort by telling me about yourself, Pilk.'

'What do you want to know?' Pilk's expression indicated that he was unlikely to confess anything.

'Who sent you and the others here yesterday to raid the ranch?'

94

'As much as I'd like to help you, it's more than my life is worth to tell you.' Pilk shook his head.

'What makes you think you're safe in our hands? You rode in here helling and shooting, and there's a woman on the spread. She could have been killed by a stray bullet. I bought into this trouble because I saw her being shot at, and I ain't gonna let you hold me up because you won't talk. You know something I need to get at, and I'll make you talk if I have to hang you up over a fire. So think about it. I'm running this show and I ain' t gonna be held back by you.'

Pilk's face slowly lost its remaining colour. His eyes filled with fear. Hilt laughed harshly.

'You know I ain't a man to be put off, huh?' he demanded. 'So what's it to be? You can tell me what I want to know and mebbe you'll still be alive when this business is settled, or you can keep your trap shut and take what you know to Hell.'

Pilk remained silent. Hilt regarded him for several moments, and the tension in the bunkhouse increased steadily. Hilt glanced at the watchful Weston.

'Light a fire back of the bunkhouse,' he said.

'You're gonna torture him?' Weston demanded.

'Sure – if he doesn't talk. But that's up to him. He can stop this any time he likes by opening up.'

'I hope you know what you're doing.' Weston turned on his heel and departed.

'Hold on there,' Pilk said unsteadily. 'Ain't you supposed to hand me over to the sheriff?'

'You'd like that, huh?' Hilt grinned. 'Catlin is a crook. He's one of the leaders in this trouble, a rustler before he took a law badge. But you know

95

that already, and now you know that I know it. I got the deadwood on Catlin, and I aim to see him through gunsmoke before too long.'

'What do you want to know?' Pilk spoke through taut lips. 'Hell, what can I tell you? I reckon you know most of it.'

'Where does Big D fit into it?' Hilt asked. 'You ride for Hank Downey, don't you?'

'Yeah. But I don't think Downey knows what is going on. His foreman, Chain Hindle, gives us our orders. We've rustled from neighbouring ranches, and brought rustled stock in across the Mexican border. There's a Mexican bandit by the name of Calvera who pushes stolen stock up across the Rio Grande from the big ranches below the border. We sell them on.'

'And what's the deal concerning Catlin and Blanchard, the banker? I heard those two are tied in with Hank Downey and plan to take over this spread, among others. Where are all the raiders coming from? They're not working on local ranches,'

'Who's been talking to you?' Pilk demanded, scowling.

'Never mind that. The men you rode in here with yesterday, they weren't part of the usual Dig D crew, huh? They were all strangers to this range.'

'That's right. Catlin is using men he used to know down along the border. They're hiding out on the range and striking when they're needed. Only a few of them have riding jobs with local ranchers.'

'Like Floyd Meeker, who rode for this brand?'

'Yeah. He's one of the rustlers. What about him?' Plik's eyes narrowed as he regarded Hilt.

'He died in town, trying to gun down Billy Ormond.'

'Did you kill him?'

'That's right. Like I'll kill a lot more of your pards before this is done.' Hilt turned on his heel and left the bunkhouse. He found Weston out back, making a pile of grass and twigs for a fire. 'Forget that,' he said. 'I got what I wanted from Pilk.'

He told the intent ramrod what he had learned, and Weston started cursing in a low tone.

'What are we gonna do?' Weston demanded.

'What would you do if you were running the show?' Hilt countered.

'I'd hit Dig D tonight and put them out of business.'

'That's what I'd like to do,' Hilt agreed. 'But we don't have enough men for the job. We can't leave the Ormonds unprotected. But give me one man to show me where Big D is and I can hit them hard when the sun comes up.'

'I'd like to go with you,' Weston said.

Hilt laughed. 'You've changed your mind about me since I rode in, huh?' he queried.

'I guess I was wrong about you.' Weston shook his head. 'I couldn't take a chance on you in case you were one of the raiders. But you've proved that you ain't.'

'You're gonna have to stick on the ranch and take care of it. And tomorrow you've got to look for Billy. Give me a good man and I'll do what's necessary.'

'Pete Bland is one of the best we got. Take him with you. I'll get him out of the bunkhouse.'

'Before we part,' Hilt said. 'Be careful of whoever

shows up here at the ranch. If Catlin comes in you can shoot him. It would be a great thing if he was taken out before the showdown.'

'You think there's gonna be a showdown?'

'You can bet your boots on it.' Hilt turned away. 'I'll throw my saddle on my buckskin. He should be raring to go now. Tell Bland to meet me over by the corral.'

He walked to the corral and found his gear. Roping the buckskin, he saddled quickly, and was waiting ready to ride when Pete Bland appeared from the bunkhouse.

'I'm mighty pleased I'm to ride with you,' Bland said.

'You might change your mind about that before tomorrow is out,' Hilt told him. 'But don't get your hopes too high. I want you to show me the way to Big D, and you'll be on your way back here before I do my stuff.'

'Heck, I'm ready to do more than that. I wanta hit someone for the way the Ormonds have been treated.'

'Saddle up and let's ride,' Hilt told him, grinning. 'We can talk it over on the way to Big D. Have you got a hatful of cartridges?'

'Sure thing. I'm loaded for bear.'

'So let's go looking for trouble.' Hilt swung into his saddle and Bland joined him. They rode off the ranch and headed south through the night, and Hilt was intent on the situation that had been thrust upon him . . .

SEVEN

Just before dawn, as the night was greying in the last minutes before the sun climbed above the horizon, Hilt dismounted on a low, brushy hill and tethered his buckskin in a straggly clump of mesquite. Pete Bland sat his mount nearby, for Hilt had told him he would be riding back to the Diamond O. The blackness of the night was fleeing before the encroaching greyness that steadily infiltrated the heavens ahead of the sun, and already to the east the horizon was taking on a lighter hue.

'Are you sure I got to ride out?' Bland demanded. 'I'd admire to stay and fight. I ain't forgetting how those buzzards came helling into the yard yesterday.'

'I do my work alone,' Hilt explained. 'You've done your job by putting me in the right place at the right time. Now ride out. You might be needed back at Diamond O. So long.'

Bland nodded and turned away. He touched spurs to his mount and went quickly. After a few minutes the sound of his departure faded, and Hilt was left alone in the vast wilderness of the open range.

Minutes later, the sun peered over the horizon and long shadows shortened quickly as daylight came to the sleeping world. By then, Hilt had drawn his Winchester from its scabbard and checked its mechanism, took a cartridge belt filled with 44.40 shells and slung it across his left shoulder, and withdrew his field-glasses from a saddle-bag. He crossed the skyline on the top of the ridge, hunkered down, and made himself comfortable. As daylight grew he peered down at the Big D cattle ranch.

Most of the buildings were of sun-dried adobe, all one-storeyed, their length and breadth making up for man's inability to make tall adobe buildings. The largest structure was obviously the ranch headquarters, standing a little apart from the two barns, two bunkhouses, the cook shack. There was a corral, a water-tank on a stilted platform, and a wind pump for raising water from a well.

The corral contained around twenty horses, and already there was a man approaching it, ready to start the day's work. Smoke was climbing lazily from a chimney on the roof of the cook shack, and men began emerging from the bunkhouses.

Hilt jacked a shell into the breech of the Winchester. He laid his field-glasses to one side and snuggled the butt of the long gun into his shoulder. At 200 yards, the ranch lay open to him, and he began to shoot rapidly, sending screeching lead around the feet of the men and putting the fear of God into them. In the space of short seconds the yard was devoid of men, and Hilt turned his attention to the water-tank, filling it with holes that spouted thin streams of water which glinted in the growing sunlight.

A big man appeared in the doorway of a small structure, and dived back into its cover when Hilt put a slug into the ground beside his left boot. Two men emerged from the ranch house, and hurried back inside when they received attention. Gunsmoke flew around Hilt, and he ducked and crawled to the right, moving before whining bullets began smacking into his vacated position. He stopped shooting and listened to the dying echoes, a taut grin on his bronzed face.

An uneasy silence settled over the ranch. Here and there, cautious men stuck up their heads to try and locate the position of the sniper. Hilt remained under cover, waiting. A man stepped into the doorway of the house, waited several moments, then moved out to the porch. He was holding a rifle in his hands, and stood gazing in Hilt's general direction. Hilt waited until the man's nerves had settled, then put a slug into the porch post close to his head.

Shooting erupted from the nearer bunkhouse and slugs came perilously close to Hilt, who returned fire until his rifle was empty. Then he ducked and reloaded the weapon from the belt he was carrying. Sweat beaded his forehead and ran into his eyes. He inched backwards, crawled into a narrow gully, then worked his way back over the skyline.

When he was in the clear he went back to the buckskin and prepared to travel, riding out to make a wide circle around Big D. North-west of the ranch, he began to quarter the area, looking for sign, and soon located the tracks of a dozen horses that seemed to have been made the day before. He followed them back towards the ranch and noted that they led right into the big, dusty yard.

He studied the ranch again. Men were moving around openly now, but with great caution. Horses were standing ready-saddled, their riders listening to orders being issued by the big man Hilt had fired at earlier. Studying the men with the aid of his glasses, Hilt watched six of them suddenly make for their broncs and ride out fast for the area from which he had sniped at them. He smiled, for they would take time to get on his trail.

When two men headed out of the gate and came in the direction where he was concealed, Hilt remounted and sat waiting in deep cover. The men passed him and rode steadily, and Hilt fell in behind and trailed them. He was hoping that those on the ranch wanted to pass on word about the shooting, and if he was right then these two riders were making for the rustling camp Pilk had mentioned.

Three hours later, the pair of riders rode into an arroyo, circling large boulders that concealed it from passers-by. A man appeared on the tallest rock, waved to the two men, and when they had passed below, vanished from sight.

Hilt tethered the buckskin in cover, took his Winchester, and sneaked towards the arroyo. Circling the rocks, he came upon the guard, who was lying in cover at the base of a rock from which he had a clear view of the approaches. He by-passed the man and went on, following the arroyo, which led into a box canyon.

A dozen horses were huddled against the canyon wall, mostly knee-hobbled to prevent their straying. A smudge of dark smoke was rising lazily from a fire, where two men were cooking a midday meal. A rough lean-to with a sod roof and open sides gave some protection from the blazing sun, and a group of men were taking advantage of its cover.

The two riders Hilt had trailed were dismounting by the lean-to, and some of the men there arose and gathered around them. Hilt used his glasses, and hard, bronzed faces came into close-up as he studied the men. Several were Mexicans wearing tall-crowned sombreros with big upturned brims. Four of the men went to their horses and saddled up, then rode out in different directions, apparently to check their surroundings.

One man, who seemed to be the leader of the band, questioned the two riders at great length, then walked under the lean-to and pointed to a man seated beside one of the poles holding up the sod roof. Hilt frowned and lifted his glasses. When he focused on the seated man he saw that it was Billy Ormond. The youngster's wrists were tied together around the pole.

The leader spoke again and the men Hilt had followed from Big D nodded. Billy was untied and thrust into a saddle. The men led him to where their horses were standing, mounted, and set off at a canter for the arroyo, taking Billy with them.

Hilt sat back in his cover and considered. That he had found the camp of the rustlers he did not doubt, and he had no intention of tackling them alone. But

Billy Ormond was another matter. He stifled a sigh and started off back to where he had left the buckskin. By the time he had sneaked by the guard, the two men taking Billy were way ahead.

Hilt checked tracks, then rode fast. Thirty minutes passed before he topped a rise and saw three riders ahead. Billy and his two captors apparently making for Big D. Riding fast, Hilt made no attempt at concealment, and he was within fifty yards of the trio when he was heard and the men swung around to face him. Slowing to a trot, Hilt approached them, a smile of welcome on his face. The two men were wary. They kept their hands close to the butts of their holstered guns but made no hostile act. Billy gazed at Hilt, then suddenly recognized him. His mouth opened, he half-grinned, then became expressionless.

'Who are you, mister?' one of the men demanded, as Hilt rode up. 'What are you doing on Big D range?'

'I've come to take Billy Ormond from you,' Hilt replied. Both men set their gunhands into motion. Hilt drew his gun and covered them before they could clear leather. They lifted their hands quickly, shocked into immobility. Hilt grinned.

'Get rid of your guns then cut Billy loose,' he directed.

'Where did you spring from?' Billy demanded, rubbing his wrists when he was free of his bonds. He disarmed the men.

'What happened to you last night after we parted?' Hilt countered.

'I was close to home when I rode into a bunch of

riders moving out a herd of our beef. They got the drop on me and took me to that rustler's roost in the canyon. One of them rode to Big D to see if I was wanted as a prisoner, and these two turned up this morning to collect me.'

'Yeah, I followed them all the way from Big D. I woke up Downey's outfit with some fancy shooting as the sun came over the hills.'

'Did you kill many of them?' Billy demanded.

Hilt shook his head. 'I wasn't in a killing mood. Just wanted them to get the feeling of being under fire. We better head back to Diamond O. Your family is a mite worried about you.'

'What about these two?' Billy was covering the two men, and looked as if he was eager to shoot them.

'Turn them loose. They can carry word to Downey that Diamond O will be visiting shortly.'

'You're the boss.' Billy motioned for the two men to depart, and they took out fast, spurring their mounts for other parts.

'How is my pa?' Billy asked, as they turned and rode on across the range.

'Better than I figured he would be. He's gonna make it.'

'What happened when you went back to town after we parted?' Billy demanded. 'We shouldn't have split up like we did.'

Hilt related his experiences, and Billy whistled through his teeth.

'Heck, you sure get things done in a hurry,' he observed. 'Funny thing, but I always had doubts about Catlin. And he paid two gunnies to plant you!

105

This crooked business has deep roots, huh? But how do we play it from here? Hey, I was forgetting! What about those two deputies we killed? Did you report them to Catlin?'

'Nope. I left them in the brush outside of town. I figured I'd done enough for one day. When I go back to get Catlin I'll explain everything then.'

'I'd like to be with you when you face Catlin,' Billy said.

They rode on at a canter, and by mid-afternoon were riding in sight of the Diamond O.

'The place looks nice and quiet,' Billy observed. 'Do you think we can beat the set-up against us?'

'We ain't done too badly so far,' Hilt replied.

They were challenged at the gate, and the guard was pleased to see Billy.

'Some of us sure had given you up for dead, Billy,' he said. 'Weston took two men out at sun-up and rode near into town looking for your body. They trailed back searching the range but couldn't find hide nor hair of you.' He looked at Hilt. 'How did you make out? Pete Bland came back right disappointed this morning, saying that you was about to take on the whole Big D crew. How many of them did you kill this time?'

'Nothing like that happened today,' Hilt said. 'And it went better than I hoped for, picking up Billy like I did.'

They rode on to the house to find Weston on the porch talking to Poggin, the killer. Sue was standing in the background by the open door. She had been talking to Poggin, but there was silence as Hilt and

Billy reined in. Billy dismounted instantly and went to Sue's side. Hilt remained in his saddle, his right hand down at his side. He held Poggin's gaze. The killer smiled easily, but his eyes were filled with cold speculation and his expression was wolfish.

'Where did you find Billy?' Weston demanded. 'I searched high and low for him between here and town.'

'I took him from the rustlers,' Hilt replied.

'Rustlers?' Poggin shrugged his wide shoulders and planted his feet firmly on the boards of the porch as if expecting trouble to flare unexpectedly.

'This is Clem Poggin,' said Sue, and despite her smile of welcome she looked tired and strained. 'Sheriff Catlin sent him here from town. Mr Poggin is looking for a job.'

'When I heard how you laid into those raiders yesterday I reckoned to throw in my hand with this outfit,' Poggin said.

'You're a stranger?' Hilt asked, and the gunman nodded. 'Did you find your pard, Kemble, before you left town?'

Poggin froze, the smile on his face becoming sickly. He opened his mouth to reply, then changed his mind and clamped his jaw shut. The fingers of his right hand twitched slightly as he readied himself for trouble.

'I was watching Catlin from the shadows when you and Kemble saw him last evening in front of the law office,' Hilt went on. 'Catlin paid you to gun me, and here you are to do the job.'

Hilt had not moved but his manner was one of

alertness. His eyes were narrowed, his attention centred on Poggin. Sue uttered a gasp, then fell silent and remained still. Weston did not move a muscle. Billy was frozen with his hand resting on the butt of his holstered gun, his eyes showing that he was ready for anything despite being aware that these two men were in a different class when it came to gun work.

'Step down off the porch,' Hilt commanded, 'then get to it, Poggin. Try and earn your money, mister.'

The silence surrounding them was filled with tension that mounted swiftly to an intolerable degree. Poggin seemed frozen by the turn of events, and moments passed before he forced his legs into motion. He stepped down from the porch and turned to face Hilt, his hands at his sides. Hilt sat the buckskin patiently, grim-lipped, unmoving like a statue, holding his reins in his left hand, his right resting close to his holstered gun.

Poggin was tall, lean and sinewy, with a prominent jaw. His close-set dark eyes were narrowed, his features wooden. There was a look of cold efficiency about him despite the unexpectedness of Hilt's challenge. He had come to Diamond O with the intention of picking the time and place for Hilt's execution, but had been disadvantaged by Hilt's awareness of him.

The strain of the silence that dragged on was intolerable. Facing each other across the space of ten feet, Hilt and Poggin looked like two hand-carved figures, their faces blank, inhuman, devoid of all expression.

'It's your play, Poggin.' Hilt's voice sounded like

rock grating on rock. 'You came here to do a job on me so get to it.'

Poggin did not move, but beads of sweat suddenly broke out on his forehead. He looked into Hilt's impassive gaze and saw death in their dark depths. The next instant he was moving, his hand darting with incredible speed to the flared butt of his holstered gun.

Yet fast as the gunman was, Hilt's instinctive reaction was swifter. His gun cleared leather and was cocked a split second ahead of Poggin. Red flame licked out from his hand and Poggin reeled backwards, clutching at his chest, his gun, uncocked, spilling from his dead hand. He fell like a tree stricken by lightning, his body raising little puffs of dust as it crashed to the yard and rolled inertly.

The crash of the shot made Sue Ormond flinch, and nausea surged through her, washing colour from her cheeks. She gasped and turned to run blindly into the house. Billy was fascinated by Hilt's impassivity, by the steely glitter in his eyes. He realized that he was not breathing, and sighed deeply, then hurried into the house behind his sister.

Art Weston pushed back his shoulders and released his pent-up breath in a long sigh. His gaze was on the prostrate figure of Clem Poggin. He looked at Hilt, who returned his gun to its holster with a slick motion, and nodded.

'It's a good thing you saw that murderous buzzard talking to Catlin last night,' he opined. 'He came in here to take pay while waiting for a chance to ventilate you. So what about Catlin? What are we gonna do about him?'

'Let him sweat until we're ready for him.' Hilt spoke curtly. 'He'll be waiting to hear from Poggin that I'm finished. Ain't he got a surprise coming?'

'What was that you said about rustlers?' Weston asked. 'Where is that camp you found Billy? Shouldn't we go talk to Downey? You said two of the Big D crew were taking Billy back to the ranch. I've always had my doubts about Big D. I reckon most of the Big D crew are in with the wideloopers.' His tone hardened and his face took on a wolfish expression. 'We should take our crew over there and put Downey out of business, permanent.'

'We need to make plans carefully,' Hilt responded.

The sound of rapidly approaching hoofs alerted Hilt and he turned to look across the yard, relaxing slowly from the high pinnacle to which the action had conveyed him. He saw Doc Errol coming in fast and was pleased to see the man. Stepping down from his saddle, he stretched and trailed his reins. Weston came off the porch.

'I'll take care of the horses over by the corral,' Weston said. 'Let me know what you reckon we should do next.'

Hilt stepped on to the porch and sat down in the rocker there. He watched the doctor come up. Errol was sweating. He dismounted in a cloud of dust and removed his Stetson to wipe his forehead. He looked at Hilt, then turned his attention to the inert figure lying in the dust.

'Don't waste your time, Doc,' Hilt said. 'He's gone

110

on to greener pastures.'

'How can you be so flippant about human life?' Errol asked. He came to the porch and stood before Hilt, who leaned back in the rocker and looked up at him.

'His name is Poggin. He came in here this morning to kill me. I don't find any pity for him in my heart.'

'He's a deputy sheriff,' Errol retorted. 'Catlin took him on last night after a flurry of killings in town.'

'That's a nasty bruise you've got on your head.'

Errol touched his forehead gingerly, wincing in pain. He sighed and sat down on the porch rail.

'There was hell to pay in town last night,' he said. 'Even I got involved. I heard a shot at the stable and was on my way there when someone laid into me with the barrel of a gun. When I woke up, Catlin was standing over me. There was a dead man in the stable, and Catlin was yelling that two of his deputies had been murdered. The blacksmith was walking his dog and the animal turned them up in the brush just outside of town. Both men had been shot in the back.'

Hilt nodded soberly. 'Catlin got any idea who put the wolf among the sheep?' he asked.

Errol shook his head. 'No one seems to know anything. Even the town drunk got trouble last night. He was found battered to death in his shack behind the Black Ace. Now who would want to lay into poor Bill Varney? Mind you, Varney's been going around town for the last couple of years, spouting about the crookedness that's building up. I suppose

111

he got a bit too near the mark and someone decided to shut his mouth.'

Hilt nodded. So Catlin had decided to put an end to Varney's accusations. He stood up, and Errol arose, shaking his head.

'How's Chuck this morning?' the doctor asked.

'Making progress, I hear,' Hilt replied.

'I'd better run my rule over him.' Errol took his medical bag from his saddlehorn and went into the house. Hilt heard his feet ascending the stairs.

Hilt glanced around the yard, then followed the doctor. He found Sue and Billy in the kitchen. The girl was distressed, and Hilt sighed as he went to her. Billy caught his eye and shook his head helplessly.

'I just don't know what life is coming to,' Sue said shakily. 'Men being killed in the yard. Cattle being rustled. It's got so we don't know who our friends are and who is against us.'

'You got some bad apples in the barrel,' Hilt said harshly, thinking that she was sorry now for taking him on the payroll. 'Get rid of them and the trouble will fade. And it's better that the men being killed are badmen and not your family. You have to protect yourself in this world, and now you're going about it the right way.'

Sue shook her head and turned to the door. 'I heard the doctor's voice, didn't I?' she asked. 'I'd better go up to him.'

Hilt watched her depart. Billy sighed heavily. The youngster's face was pale but there was nothing wrong with his determination.

112

'What happens next?' he asked eagerly. 'Do we ride into town and finish off Catlin?'

'I don't think it is going to be as easy as that,' Hilt replied. 'Things being what they are, I expect another attack to come in against the ranch, and we better get ready for it.'

As he finished speaking a shot hammered echo-ingly outside and a bullet struck the front of the house . . .

EIGHT

Hilt grasped Billy's shoulder as the youngster made for the door, restraining him. He lifted his gun from its holster. More shots sounded. Hilt passed Billy, admonishing him.

'Stay in here and make sure no one gets into the house,' he warned. 'You've got a family to worry about, Billy.'

Billy bared his teeth in a mirthless grin and his shoulders slumped. He remained standing at the bottom of the stairs, his gun upraised in his hand.

'Let them try to come in,' he said, as Hilt hurried out.

Peering out the doorway, Hilt saw gunsmoke blossoming at least a hundred yards out from the yard. He nodded. No doubt this was in reply to his attack at Big D. He saw Weston by the corral, hunched over, gun in hand, watching the snipers. There were men in the bunkhouse ready for trouble, the muzzles of their rifles showing at the windows.

A bullet struck the porch by the doorway, close to Hilt's head, splintering wood. He eased back. These men were not content to just shoot up the place. They wanted blood. He cursed because Weston had taken the buckskin over to the corral, and with it had gone his field-glasses and rifle. He contented himself with looking around, trying to pinpoint the positions of the four or five gunnies shooting up the place.

Weston suddenly sprang into the saddle he had put on his roan and went at a gallop across the yard and out through the gate. The guard was crouched in cover there but holding his fire. Hilt cursed, for it seemed to him that the ramrod was being foolhardy to an extreme. Those riflemen were just waiting for a foray against them. But Weston seemed to bear a charmed life. All the rifles out there fired at him but missed, and the ramrod eventually vanished into a draw and the shooting ceased.

But the snipers returned to firing at the ranch, and Hilt clenched his teeth and waited out the storm. A rifle started shooting at the rear of the house and Hilt ran to the foot of the stairs and called for Billy. The youngster replied from upstairs.

'There are men coming in from the rear,' Billy warned.

'Stay up there and cover me,' Hilt replied. 'I'm going out the back way so don't shoot me.'

He hurried into the kitchen where the house-keeper was hiding in a corner, grasping a rifle, scared but determined.

'Don't shoot at me by mistake,' Hilt told her in passing, and she smiled, shaking her head emphatically.

115

He jerked open the back door, stepping to one side as he did so. A bullet hummed in his ear, crossed the kitchen and slammed against a tin pot with a metallic clang. Hilt sprang outside and dived to the ground as a string of shots came at him. He moved fast, and the bullets thudded harmlessly behind him. Drawing his Colt, he made for the well out back and gained its shelter, hunkering down and cocking his pistol.

Four riders were galloping around out back, firing at windows, and any target that took their fancy. They were at close range, and Hilt lifted his pistol and began firing rapidly. He did not seem to aim. He saw movement and fired, emptying the gun quickly. When he ducked to reload his empty chambers, two of the four gunman had pitched out of their saddles and the other two were hightailing it back to a safer distance.

Hilt went back into the house. Gun echoes were dying away, growling in the distance. He went to the front of the house and looked across the yard. Art Weston was riding back through the gateway, reloading his pistol. Hilt went out to the porch and waited for Weston to arrive.

The foreman came up and dismounted, his expression filled with defiance. He was sweating, and removed his Stetson to wipe his forehead.

'That was a damnfool play,' Hilt observed. 'You were asking to get yourself killed.'

'A man can take only so much,' Weston growled. 'I can't stand around while hardcases ride in here doing what they like. Anyway, I chased them off. I saw them hightailing it back towards Big D.'

'Did you recognize any of them?' Hilt asked.

'They were too far away.' Weston shook his head. 'It's good enough that they left. Was there shooting out back?'

'Four came in that way. I nailed two of them.'

'We'd better take a look at them.' Weston sighed heavily as he crossed the porch and entered the house.

Hilt followed and they went out back. Weston examined the two men. Both were dead, and strangers. The ramrod was still shaking his head when he straightened and looked at Hilt.

'It's a funny thing that all these raiders are strangers,' he mused. 'What happens now? We can't just sit around waiting for another attack. One of these times they may get lucky.'

'Have you got enough men to mount a raid against Big D?' Hilt asked. 'You'd need to leave maybe six men behind to defend the spread.'

Weston shook his head. 'I got twelve men all told, and they're cowpokes, not gunmen. They'd do pretty well defending the place, but they ain't the men to take out on a raid against seasoned rustlers and hell raisers.'

'It wouldn't help much to do that,' Hilt said. 'In a case like this it would be better to go for the men running the business. Cut off the head of a snake and the rest of it dies.'

Weston nodded. 'One thing I've learned to do over the past day is listen to you,' he said. 'You got anything in mind?'

'I reckon the most dangerous man in all this is Catlin, and he should be high on the list for removal.'

'Yeah, I've already come to that conclusion. But he's the sheriff. You can't just ride into town and kill him. He's got some tough deputies around Cedar Creek, and the whole town would back him. Then we'd be shooting at honest men who believe they are doing the right thing.'

'I wouldn't go at the job that bull-headed. I know Catlin is a bad 'un so I wouldn't have a second thought about killing him. But a better way to deal with him is get him fired from his job. Then he'd be just an ordinary man and we could handle him.'

'You'd need to convince the mayor in town that Catlin is crooked.' Weston shook his head. 'Cy Forrest. He's also the local land agent. But I got suspicions about him. If I had to pick someone in town I thought was wrong I'd go for Forrest, without hesitation.'

'Yeah, that's the risk we'd be running, going to someone already on Catlin's side.' Hilt suppressed a sigh. 'I guess my way is the best. I'll ride into town and call out Catlin. With him dead you'll be able to concentrate on the badmen on the range. I'll need someone to go with me who knows Cedar Creek and the townsmen.'

'I'll ride with you.' Weston spoke without hesitation. 'I can't take much more of this standing around while others get all the excitement.'

'You got someone you can leave in charge who can

do a good job of defending the place and keeping Billy in check?'

'Sure. Pete Bland is a good man. I'll have a word with him. But I don't expect another attack here. They ain't doing nothing but losing men. I'll be ready to ride in fifteen minutes.'

Hilt watched the ramrod go off across the yard until Sue spoke to him from the doorway at his back.

'Is it safe to come out now?' she asked.

'I think they've gone for the moment,' he replied, turning to her and smiling. 'But it will never be safe to stand around out here until the war has been won.'

'What are you going to do now?'

'I'm planning another jaunt to town, and Weston is going with me this time. All you need to do is keep Billy on the ranch. Knee hobble him, if you have to. I don't want to come back and hear that he's taken off on some fool business.'

'Billy won't be going anywhere,' she said firmly.

'Has the doctor finished?' Hilt asked. 'I'm wondering if he's gonna ride back to town. I'd like to question him, and if we can ride together it will save me time.'

'He's getting ready to leave, and I think he said he was heading back to town. Is there anything you need before you ride out? You left the ranch in the middle of the night, and as far as I know, you haven't eaten a thing since yesterday.'

'I won't be able to get anything in town when I ride in,' Hilt mused, smiling ruefully. 'I'll be too busy for that.'

'Come into the kitchen and I'll get you something. Doc Errol is having coffee, and he'll be glad of company to town.'

Hilt followed the girl into the kitchen and sat down at the table opposite Errol. The doctor smiled.

'You're doing better than I thought you would,' he observed. 'But one man can't fight an army, and that's what you've got facing you. There are a lot of men in town who are against law and order, and the range seems overcrowded with gunnies and hard cases all out to make a crooked dollar.'

'I reckon you're the man to fill me in on the background of folks in town,' Hilt said. 'I'll ride with you when you're ready and you can give me the lowdown on the men running the place.'

'You've got proof against Catlin, I hear.' Errol's face was grave. 'There's no chance of getting him out of office. He's dug himself in pretty deep over the past two years.'

'I agree with you.' Hilt nodded. 'Catlin is gonna face me through gunsmoke soon as I hit town. He's a problem.'

Errol half rose from the table in alarm. 'Heck, that's cold-blooded, even for you,' he declared. 'You can't do it like that. The minute you kill Catlin while he's wearing the sheriff's badge you'll brand yourself an outlaw, no matter what he's done.'

'I ain't got time for niceties.' Hilt shook his head. 'But I won't stand in the street and call Catlin out. We can entice him into a lonely spot and take him prisoner if you think that would be a better way. But he should be dead. He can't make mischief in Hell.'

'Let's think about it on the ride to town.' Errol got to his feet. 'I'll be on the porch, ready to ride, when you're through in here.'

Hilt watched the doctor's tall figure leave the kitchen and decided that the medical man spoke a lot of good sense. He sat mulling over the situation as he knew it, and when Sue put a plate of food before him he ate hungrily, aware that he would not know where or when his next meal would come from. Hot coffee topped him up and he was eager to ride when he arose from the table.

'Be careful in town,' Sue warned him, and he grinned.

'What else?' he countered. 'Careful is my middle name.'

'What is your name? How did you come to be called Hilt?'

'It's short for Hilton.' He went out to the porch.

Art Weston was waiting with Doc Errol. The ramrod had saddled a fresh horse for Hilt and transferred his gear to the animal. Weston mounted his roan and the doctor swung up into his saddle on a chestnut mare. Hilt liked the look of the grey horse that Weston had picked for him and he mounted quickly and turned for the gate.

Once on the trail for town they settled into a lope that covered the ground fast without tiring the horses unduly. Hilt rode on the doctor's right side and Weston followed a couple of lengths to the rear. The afternoon was almost past and the heat from the westering sun baked them with its intensity.

'Before you fill me in on Catlin, Doc,' Hilt said, 'let

121

me tell you that he paid two gunnies to kill me.'

Errol's seamed face evinced surprise. He shook his head in disbelief as he looked at Hilt.

'Yeah.' Hilt nodded. 'It takes some believing, I know. But before Catlin became the sheriff here he was a big-time rustler elsewhere. He came here to get the job as sheriff in order to set himself up for a big operation of rustling and land-stealing.'

Errol was silent for a long time, evidently mulling over what he had been told. Then he nodded.

'I guess what you say does clear up some points about Catlin that have bothered me from the moment I first met him. Thinking of what poor Bill Varney used to say about Catlin and some of the others, I can believe now that he was telling the truth when we all used to take his words with a pinch of salt.'

'I spoke with Varney before he was killed by Catlin.'

'You saw Catlin kill Varney?'

'I didn't see it happen, but I got to Varney after he struck you down outside the stable.'

'Varney did that?' Errol frowned. 'But go on. What did you see?'

'Catlin and a deputy trapped me in Varney's shack. I killed the deputy and got away. As I left I saw Catlin going into Varney's place. And you told me that Varney was found dead. What more proof do you need?'

'There was some trouble after Catlin had been a deputy sheriff for a few months,' Doc Errol commented. 'His predecessor, Sheriff Benton, was shot in the back. That was when Catlin took over the office; Benton's killer was never found.'

'Are there any of the men running the town who seem to be particularly friendly with Catlin? Varney hinted that he was fired from his job at the bank because he learned too much of what was going on.'

'Tom Blanchard is the banker, and was a staunch supporter of Catlin's bid to be the new sheriff.' Errol looked doubtful for a moment. 'It makes you wonder just who is in cahoots with the badmen. But some-one is making a fortune out of the rustling that's going on. I've heard it said more than once, and by men who should know what they're talking about, that much of the rustling is done by a gang of Mexican bandits. We're close enough to the border to make that feasible. But the Texas Rangers haven't been able to come up with any proof of that, and they're always riding around. I've talked with Captain Clarke of Company B a number of times. I see him often, when his men have been shot. Now he'd be very interested in what you have to say about Catlin being crooked. Maybe I should get word to Clarke to come in and talk to you.'

Hilt smiled and shook his head. 'I don't think anything a two-bit gunhand has to say will interest the Texas Rangers.'

'Are you wanted anywhere for breaking the law?' Errol looked into Hilt's eyes. 'It's all too easy for a man living by the gun to fall foul of the law.'

'I'm not wanted by the law,' Hilt said. 'Mind you, it's a different matter with friends or relatives of men I have killed. To my knowledge there are at least three men hunting me for shooting someone, and on my part, I'm hoping to get my sights on Buck Dunne.'

'I've heard that name! Dunne robbed a bank in Bitter Creek a few miles north of here only a couple of weeks ago. They said he was making for the border.'

'I killed his two brothers, both outlaws, who killed my brother. I won't be satisfied until I've seen Buck Dunne through gunsmoke.'

They rode in silence for some minutes, and Hilt used the time to think over the problems he was facing. He needed to get back to his personal war with Dunne, but, having taking up his gun on behalf of the Ormonds, he would continue to fight their enemies until it was over.

The afternoon had passed by the time they reached Cedar Creek, and Hilt reined in as soon as he sighted the huddled buildings of the street.

'I can't ride in openly,' he said. 'I need a free hand, and if Catlin arrests me then I'll be no more use to Diamond O.'

'I'll ride in with Doc and look around to see how the wind is blowing,' Weston said. 'I'll let you know if Catlin is on the prod for you.'

Hilt shook his head. 'That don't come across as the way I should handle it. We'll ride in. I'll play it as she comes.'

Doc Errol shook his head disapprovingly but made no further comment. He shook his reins and went on, entering the street and riding steadily along its length, heading for the livery barn at the far end. Hilt and Weston rode together, and Hilt's hand was close to the butt of his gun as he looked around.

As they passed the law office, Hilt tensed and watched for signs of Catlin.

'I ought to drop in on Catlin right now,' he said. 'If I don't face him down he could get the drop on me, and I reckon back-shooting must be his favourite pastime.'

He turned instantly and rode to the hitching rail in front of the office despite Weston's protests. Dismounting, he wrapped his reins around the rail and stepped up to the sidewalk. Weston joined him quickly, and Hilt glanced around the almost deserted street.

'Seems to be quiet around here,' Weston commented.

'More than usual?' Hilt grinned and adjusted his gunbelt. 'I guess we can soon change that, huh?' His fingers brushed the butt of his gun as he pushed open the door of the office and stepped inside.

The interior of the office was gloomy. An oldish man sat at a battered desk situated to catch the light from an alley window, and he looked up quickly at their entrance. Weston stepped up beside Hilt and spoke quickly.

'Hi, Jake. Is Catlin around?'

'Nope. He rode out earlier with a posse. Got word that Buck Dunne, the outlaw, was seen over by Boulder Rock and went after him. Dunne hit a bank in the county a couple of weeks ago. The word is that he's headed for Mexico with his loot.'

Hilt tensed at the news, his lips pulling tight. Jake was regarding him while delivering the information about the sheriff.

'New man on your payroll, Art?' he queried.

'Yeah. It pays to keep up with the times.' Weston sounded uneasy, and Hilt shot him a quick glance. 'When is Catlin expected back?'

'Not for several days. They took supplies for a week in case Dunne gives them the slip. What you wanta see Catlin about?'

'More trouble at Diamond O. Another bunch of gunslicks rode in and tried to shoot us up.'

Jake tut-tutted and leaned back in his seat, getting comfortable for a long chat. Hilt moved impatiently but contained himself, needing to be brought up to date on local events.

'I don't know what this place is coming to,' Jake mused. 'You think you've got trouble! Heck, we've had more than our share these past coupla days. They found two deputies, Toll and Yelding, dead, just out of town. Both shot in the back. The word is that one of your riders nailed them.'

'One of mine?' Weston shook his head. 'I doubt it.'

'Blaine, Frank Blaine. Catlin plans to swing by your place, if he don't get Dunne, and pick up Blaine.'

'When did this happen?' Weston's voice tremored.

'Last night. And Bill Varney was found battered to death in his shack.'

'And Blaine did that too, huh?' Weston laughed. 'Well, I'll tell you that Blaine and Billy came on back to the ranch when they left town yesterday, and

Billy didn't say nothing about any trouble.'

'They say that Blaine is hell on wheels with his gun. He got Ben Hussey from a standing start, and Hussey was using his quick-fire rig. Busted Hussey's arm, and put him out of action for the rest of the year, I shouldn't wonder.'

'Hussey's been asking for it a long time.' Weston turned to leave. He glanced at Hilt. 'Come on, Smith. We'll go get ourselves a beer. I reckoned the town looked quiet, Jake. How many men rode out in the posse?'

'Fifteen, mebbe. Catlin reckons Dunne is heading a tough gang since his brothers were killed.'

'Watch out they don't sneak in here while Catlin is away,' Weston retorted. 'They might have plans for our bank.'

Hilt was thoughtful as they left the office. So Buck Dunne was still around, and he was too busy to get on the outlaw's trail. He hoped the posse would fail. He wanted Dunne for himself.

'What happens now?' Weston demanded. 'With Catlin out of town, it looks like we've had our ride for nothing.'

'Maybe not. Let's get that drink you mentioned. I wanta look up Hussey and ask him why he was so keen to gun down Billy.'

'Hussey has a big set-up in the Black Ace,' Weston warned. 'If you've put him out of action he'll be itching to see you again, and this time he'll be ready for you.'

Hilt nodded. 'The town looks quiet,' he observed. 'Maybe too quiet. Let's liven it up a little. If we give

Hussey some grief there's no telling what might flare up.'

'Anything you say,' Weston responded. 'I just hope you know what you're doing.'

Hilt eased his gun in its holster as they went along the sidewalk to the Black Ace saloon, and they were still several yards from the batwings when a man carrying a rifle emerged from the building and lifted his weapon into the aim. Hilt reacted instantly. His Colt appeared in his hand and he fired a split second before the rifle opened up, his bullet taking the rifleman in the throat. The rifle cracked but the man was already dead and, as his bullet ploughed into the boardwalk a couple of feet from Weston's right boot, he fell lifeless while the echoes of the shooting fled across the uneasy town.

NINE

Hilt dashed forward as the echoes of the shooting faded and shouldered open the batwings, his gun lifting to cover the interior of the saloon. He found several men inside, all frozen into inactivity by the sudden shots. There was a 'tender behind the bar, held in the act of wiping glasses. A cowboy stood at the bar, a glass in his hand raised to his lips, and four men were seated at a gaming table, all still, heads swivelled to look at the door.

Hilt paused, gun steady. He heard Weston enter the saloon at his back, the batwings creaking.

'Art, cover the men at the table,' Hilt rapped, and walked to the bar. The 'tender set down the glass he was wiping, his eyes on Hilt's gun.

'Who was the man with the rifle?' Hilt demanded.

'Uh, Sam Patten. He works here as a shotgun guard.'

'That's what I figured. Why was he carrying a rifle?'

'We heard that Buck Dunne is in the county.' The 'tender glanced over at the gaming table where four men were motionless under the threat of Weston' s gun. 'The boss is over there. Maybe he can tell you what's going on. I don't know nothing.'

Hilt glanced towards the table, and his lips compressed when he saw Ben Hussey there. The gambler's right arm was heavily bandaged and in a sling. His fleshy face was ashen, and it was obvious that he was still suffering from shock.

A tall, thin, fair-haired man at the table lifted a hand to attract Hilt's attention. 'I'm Ike Carmel,' he said. 'I own this place. Did you kill Patten?'

Hilt crossed the room to the table, his heels rapping on the sanded boards. His gun was pointing at no one in particular, but each man felt that it was covering him.

'Patten's dead,' Hilt said without emotion. 'Why did he start shooting at me without warning? Acting on orders?'

'Not my orders, if he was,' Carmel said quickly.

The saloon owner was middle-aged and smartly dressed in a dark suit. He had an air of sleekness about him, and looked scrupulously clean, as if he had just stepped out of a bath. His hair was flat on his head, heavily greased and with not a hair out of place. His face was lean, hard, with the eyes of a wolf.

'Someone gave him orders,' Hilt insisted, 'or he wouldn't have stepped out through the batwings and let fly at me without warning. He must have been watching for me in particular.'

'It's beyond me.' Carmel shook his head.

'No matter.' Hilt waggled the gun slightly. 'I came

in to talk to Hussey.' His incisive gaze switched to the fleshy gambler. 'Tell me why you were so keen to gun down Billy Ormond last night? You baited him until he lost his temper, and then drew on him with that quick-fire rig of yours. You didn't give him a chance. If I hadn't been there, Billy would have died. I could see what was happening.'

'It wasn't like that.' Hussey's voice was ragged. 'Billy was on the prod the moment he came into the saloon. He was fired up by the attack on his father, and said he was looking for the men who did it.'

'Billy wouldn't have said that.' Hilt shook his head. 'He saw one of the two men dead before he left the ranch to come in for the doctor, and knew I was riding out after the other. I know a set-up when I see it, and Billy was like a calf going to the slaughter when I walked into the saloon.'

'I'm telling the truth,' Hussey rapped.

'You're a liar. I'd rather believe my eyes, and I wouldn't take the word of a two-bit gambler who looks like he'd gyp his own mother at the tables.'

Hussey flared instantly. His face reddened and his dark eyes brightened. He made as if to get to his feet, then waved his injured hand helplessly and subsided.

'If I wasn't handicapped I'd call you out,' he snarled. 'I don't take that kind of talk from any man. You ain't got no call to come in here and accuse me of plotting murder.'

'I'll let it drop for now,' Hilt told him. 'But if I'm still around when you're all healed up I'll come look-ing for you. Better than that, I reckon you should get

131

out of town before dark. I'll be around, and if I see you after five I'll kill you.'

'You're running me out?' Hussey pushed himself upright. His face had paled even more and he looked scared.

'Yeah, and you better get moving now. I got your measure and I'll be looking for you.'

Hussey gazed at Hilt with rage smouldering in his eyes. Then he turned and walked to the stairs leading up to the rooms over the saloon. His left boot squeaked slightly with each step and the sound was loud in the tense silence.

Hilt looked at the two men still at the table with Carmel. One was small and dark, dressed in a store suit with a string tie around his neck. The third man was big and fleshy, also wearing a store suit, and he looked prosperous. He was sweating badly and seemed apprehensive. He was still holding cards in his hands, and they were shaking slightly.

'Who are your friends, Carmel?' Hilt demanded.

The saloon owner jerked a thumb at the smaller man, who was regarding Hilt with narrowed eyes and a deadpan expression on his weasel face.

'This is Cy Forrest, the land agent. He's also town mayor. That's Tom Blanchard opposite, who owns the bank.'

Hilt nodded. 'I had a mighty interesting talk with Bill Varney last night before he was killed,' he said. 'What he told me puts you in a bad light, Blanchard.'

'You can't pay heed to the inane ramblings of a drunk,' Blanchard retorted. 'I fired Varney in the first place because he drank too much and didn't do

132

his job properly. His behaviour after that proved I did the right thing.'

Weston's gun blasted twice in quick succession. Hilt glanced around as gunsmoke plumed across the saloon. Weston was pointing his gun up the stairs, and the next instant Hussey's big body came tumbling down. The gambler thudded on the bottom stair and lay on his back, eyes wide and staring, a pistol clutched in a death-grip in his left hand.

'He was fixing to plug you,' Weston said harshly. 'But I reckoned he might try a snake-trick like that so I was watching for him. This place is a nest of rattlers. It wouldn't surprise me if the trouble going on around the county is hatched out right in here.'

Hilt smiled and holstered his pistol. 'You could be right at that, Art. But the rats will take some smoking out, huh? Let's have that drink we promised ourselves. This sure is thirsty work.'

'Have it on the house.' Carmel started to his feet.

'Stay out of it,' Hilt warned, and the saloonman sat down again. Hilt walked to the bar and ordered two beers. Weston joined him, still holding his pistol. Hilt slapped a silver coin on the bar.

Weston laid his .45 on the bar top. The 'tender set up two beers and faded into the background. The silence in the low building was overwhelming.

'There's something I meant to talk to you about,' Hilt said, after swallowing a mouthful of beer. 'When Billy and me left the saloon last night a Diamond O ranny by the name of Floyd Meeker took a shot at Billy.'

'Billy mentioned it.' Weston buried his nose in his

glass, almost draining it, then wiped his mouth with the back of his left hand as he set the glass back on the bar. 'I don't know what Meeker was doing in town. As far as I knew he was riding the line to the north. I figure we could have some of the rustlers in the crew, and I've been thinking about that, looking for unusual behaviour in anyone that might point to their guilt. It's the hell of a note when you can't trust your own crew.'

'Is there anyone you suspect of leading a double life?'

'I ain't come up with anything yet, but I sure am watching points.' Weston picked up his pistol and reloaded the empty chambers. You know, with Catlin out of town, I think we're wasting our time around here. Why don't we ride out and track down the posse? We only have the jailer's word for it that Catlin is out after the outlaw. He could be raising hell someplace, and if we could get the deadwood on him we can put an end to his game.'

'A good idea.' Hilt nodded. He glanced at the batwings as they were pushed open, but relaxed when Doc Errol entered in a hurry. 'Let's get out of here, huh?'

Errol hurried to the bottom of the stairs and bent over the prostrate Hussey. He barely checked the man before straightening to look at Hilt and Weston. Errol seemed tired and harassed, his eyes looking as if they had not been closed in a week.

'Hussey is dead,' Errol said.

'I could have told you that,' Weston grinned. 'I shot him. He was fixing to shoot Blaine.'

Hilt went to the batwings and the ramrod followed him. They left the saloon and walked back along the sidewalk to where their horses were standing at the rail in front of the law office.

'The posse rode out this morning,' Hilt mused. 'We need to know what direction they took. Have a word with that jailer and see if you can get something out of him worth a damn.'

Weston nodded and went into the law office. Hilt stood on the sidewalk with his back to the front wall of the office, his keen eyes busy watching the street. He drew his pistol, checked it, then slid it back into its holster. As he did so he heard the pounding of approaching hoofs coming into town. He looked around quickly but saw nothing, and then about ten riders came galloping out of an alley to the right, and ten more appeared on the left, emerging from another alley and converging on the law office from two sides.

Hilt stood with his hands at his sides. The odds were too great for him to resist and he awaited developments. His keen gaze probed the newcomers, who reined in and sat covering him with drawn pistols, and he felt a strand of relief when he failed to spot Catlin among them.

A tall, heavily built man of around fifty stepped down from the saddle of a big grey horse and came on to the sidewalk, his keen gaze on Hilt's face. He moved with assurance, a fixed smile on his craggy features.

'Howdy?' he greeted. 'Is Sheriff Catlin inside?'

'Nope. He left town with a posse this morning,'

Hilt replied. 'I was hoping to see him myself.'

The door of the office was opened and Art Weston appeared. He looked around at the motionless riders, then glanced at the man confronting Hilt.

'Captain Clarke,' he said, grinning. 'Am I glad to see you!'

'Howdy, Art.' Captain Clarke shook hands with the Diamond O ramrod. 'I admit that you were right after all about who is behind the rustling. We've just had a run-in with a bunch of Mex rustlers who were pushing four, mebbe five hundred head of wetbacks on to Big D. We shot the hell out of them, and Hank Downey and his Big D crew didn't like it one little bit when they showed while we were mopping up the Mexes. So Downey's dead, as are most of his crew, and before Downey died he confessed to helping run the rustling in Morgan County. He put the deadwood on some of the men here in town who are mixed up in the trouble, and you'll be surprised to learn that Sheriff Catlin figures high on the list.'

'We ain't surprised, Captain,' Weston said. 'Me and Smith came in to try and nail Catlin. We got evidence against him. Among other things, he paid a killer named Poggin to kill Smith.'

'The hell you say! Poggin is a wanted outlaw with a price on his head. He rode with Buck Dunne. Where is Poggin now?'

'Dead. Smith outdrew him. He's lying back of the bunkhouse on Diamond O.'

Because of what he had learned, Captain Clarke was eyeing Hilt closely. 'You must be almighty fast with your gun if you outdrew Poggin,' he said. 'Are you wanted by the law?'

'No.' Hilt shook his head.

'I could use a man like you.' Clarke looked around. 'We'll talk later. Right now, I got some more rounding up to do. Ben Hussey for a start, and Cy Forrest, and even Tom Blanchard, the banker. Seems they're all in the swim for unlawful profit.'

'We just left that trio in the Black Ace with Ike Carmel,' Weston said, grinning. 'But Hussey is dead.'

'You again, Smith?' Captain Clarke asked.

'Not this time.' Weston dropped a hand to his gun. 'I nailed that buzzard as he was fixing to shoot Smith.'

Hilt listened, unable to believe this development. Captain Clarke sent pairs of Rangers along the street with orders to pick up the men Downey had named, then led the way into the law office. He ousted the jailer from his seat behind the desk and dropped into it, motioning for the jailer to stand before him.

'Jake, where has Catlin taken the posse?' Clarke asked.

'I don't know, Captain. Catlin ain't one to talk of his doings. He rode out in hurry after a Big D rider came in. There must be something wrong on the range for Catlin to take a posse. He usually rides alone.'

'And you didn't hear what the Big D rider said?'

'Something about Big D getting shot up at sunrise.'

'That was my doing.' Hilt explained his actions of

the morning and how he had rescued Billy Ormond from the rustlers. Clarke sat up straight in his seat when he learned of the rustler hideout in the canyon north of Big D.

'Heck, we've been looking for just such a place,' he said eagerly. 'I've suspected for some time that Calvera, the Mexican bandit, has been roosting on this side of the border when he's buying or selling cattle over here.'

'I did see some Mexicans in the canyon but I didn't take much notice of them,' Hilt said. 'I was keen to get Billy Ormond away.'

'We better ride pronto and take a look around that spot.' Clarke pushed himself to his feet. 'Show us the way, Smith. We'll stop off at the stable in case Joe Ketchum can tell us which way Catlin rode out with his posse. It's possible he's gone in the same direction.'

Hilt nodded, but his interest in the local situation had waned since he'd heard that Buck Dunne was somewhere around.

'Art, you can do me a favour,' Clarke said, as he headed for the street. 'Take over here as the tempo-rary sheriff until we nail Catlin. Get some towns-men to back you. If Catlin shows up again, give him a hot reception, but take him alive for me if you can.'

'I ought to be getting back to Diamond O,' Weston replied, as they emerged from the office. 'If Catlin shows up there with his posse then there could be hell to pay. Someone has been intent on killing the Ormonds and grabbing the ranch.'

'The hell you say!' Clarke nodded. 'All right, I'll

leave a couple of my men behind to handle local law.'

'Thanks.' Weston went to his roan and swung into the saddle. 'I'll see you back at the ranch when you've finished with the Rangers, Smith,' he said.

'Sure thing.' Hilt watched the ramrod wheel his mount and ride off along the street. He went to his buckskin and prepared the animal for travel, waiting on Captain Clarke to finish making his arrangements.

Two of the Rangers dismounted and prepared to remain in town. There was movement along the street, and Hilt saw Rangers coming towards the office, surrounding half-a-dozen men who had been taken prisoner. He saw Ike Carmel, Forrest and Blanchard and the bartender, all protesting vociferously as they were being ushered along the street. Clarke was giving final orders to the Rangers who would stay behind.

'Pick up the rest of the men I've named and hold them until we get back. Watch out for Catlin coming back. From what I hear, he's as slick as pailful of rattlers.'

The two Rangers nodded and accompanied the prisoners into the office. Clarke signalled to the rest of his company and they mounted and rode along the street to the stable. Hilt was content to just ride along. This was out of his hands now, but so long as he was in at the kill he did not mind.

The liveryman was in his yard in front of the barn, forking straw off a wagon into the loft. He paused and leaned on his pitchfork when Clarke hailed him.

'No,' he said, in reply to Clarke's question. 'Catlin

didn't tell me where he was riding. He headed out south but switched direction just before I lost sight of him. Looked to me like he cut away towards Big D.'

Clarke waved a hand and led the Rangers on. One of the men rode out in front by a few yards and checked the trail. An excellent tracker, he soon found the place where the posse had turned off and got down to study sign. A few minutes later he turned to report to Clarke.

'I count more than a dozen horses,' he said, 'riding close together and travelling fast. Looks like they wanted to get somewhere in a hurry. One set of tracks belongs to that big black stallion Catlin rides. I'd know the prints of that son of Satan anywhere.'

'Follow them,' Clarke said grimly.

They rode on through the gathering evening. In his mind's eye, Hilt visualized the route he had taken that morning, using his fine sense of direction, and estimated that they were south-east of the canyon where he had rescued Billy Ormond and roughly twenty miles away. He relayed the information to Clarke.

'Looks like we're heading in that direction now,' Clarke observed. 'We ain' t gonna reach the canyon before dark so I reckon to make camp at a creek a few miles ahead and go on in the morning so as to reach the canyon before sun-up. I don't have much hope of catching anyone there now. What happened today will have scared off the rustlers. But we can pick up tracks there and follow on.'

They reached the creek late in the day and made

cold camp, more to rest their horses than them-
selves. After two hours' rest, they set out again, and
before dawn, when the sky was greying and the
quarter-moon had waned, Hilt, who had moved
ahead with Captain Clarke, reined up in cover just
out from the rocks guarding the arroyo that gave
access to the hidden canyon.

Hilt followed the course of the arroyo at a
distance, until the wide sweep of the canyon
opened up before them. The sun was beginning to
show above the eastern horizon, chasing out the
shadows and increasing their range of vision.
When Captain Clarke saw the camp there were
two men already raking the fire and making breakfast.

'I count fifteen horses in that corral down there,'
Clarke said. 'Still too dark to make out details, but
I'd know Catlin' s black stallion a mile away, and I
don't think it's down there. Stay here, Smith, and
keep watch. I'll bring up my men and we'll surround
this place before we strike.'

Hilt nodded and settled down, content to wait.

As the minutes passed and the sun came up, Hilt
could see the men in the canyon rousing out of their
blankets. The majority of them were wearing
sombreros, and Hilt did not see Catlin's black stallion in the corral. But there was no time to muse
over the situation. Captain Clarke came back with
his Rangers and bellied down on the rim of the
canyon to make an appreciation.

'I can recognize Calvera down there,' Clarke said
eagerly. 'That tall Mexican sitting by the camp-fire.

141

That's Calvera. I've been trying to catch him this side of the border but he's always been too sharp for that. Now we've got him.'

Clarke slid back from the rim and issued orders to his men. Four dismounted, taking their rifles, and moved to the left to cut off any retreat to the arroyo.

'Wait until we're moving in on them before you cut loose, unless they get wind of us and take off. I'll take the rest of the men down into the canyon and attack them from the right. Any that run will make for the arroyo so you can get them. Smith, I think you'd better stay here and watch the attack.'

Hilt nodded and fetched his rifle and belt of cartridges. He joined the four Rangers at the spot where the arroyo met the canyon and hunkered down in a good position. The canyon tapered at this end into the arroyo, and he was satisfied that any rustlers trying to escape would become sitting ducks for the deadly rifles covering the area.

Full daylight came and the rustler camp was filled with bustle. Breakfast was being eaten, and all the horses were ready saddled for travel. Minutes dragged by, and Hilt began to think the rustlers would be riding out before Captain Clarke and his men sprang the trap.

Then he saw a line of horsemen coming into view in the canyon itself, moving at a canter towards the camp below. Hilt jacked a shell into the breech of his Winchester and prepared for action. One of the rustlers spotted the oncoming riders and raised the alarm. The next instant guns were banging, and the

Rangers swept forward at a gallop, yipping and yelling, to ram their special kind of law down the throats of the badmen.

TEN

The rustlers responded to the Ranger attack with surprising speed, returning fire with pistols or rifles, and an intense battle flared. A Ranger beside Captain Clarke suddenly reeled and then fell backward out of his saddle. Three rustlers dropped in their tracks. The line of Rangers thundered into the camp, guns blazing furiously, and more men dropped on both sides.

But the rustlers were shaken by the surprise of the attack and soon broke away, running for their horses. Gunfire rolled and echoed across the canyon and, as the rustlers streamed toward the arroyo – their rat-hole of escape – Hilt and the four Rangers on the rim prepared to take a hand.

Eight rustlers came galloping under their waiting guns, and Hilt saw that the foremost was the Mexican Clarke had identified as Calvera. He drew a bead on the man, swung his rifle to allow for movement, and squeezed the trigger. Calvera jerked under the deadly impact of the 44.40 slug and slumped over the neck of his horse. The other

Rangers opened fire, and in the space of five seconds all the rustlers were down. Two immediately sprang up and began running for cover, and Hilt shot one of them through the back of the neck. The other dropped as quickly, like a blade of grass caught by a scythe.

Looking around, Hilt saw that none of the rustlers had escaped the trap, and he joined the four Rangers when they descended into the canyon, using a game trail.

By the time they reached the camp-fire, Captain Clarke had restored order. The Rangers were collecting the bodies of dead rustlers, and five wounded Mexicans were taken prisoner. One Ranger was dead and six had received wounds, but Clarke was pleased with the outcome of their venture.

'I've been after Calvera for years,' he declared, 'and never would have believed he could be trapped so easily. He's always given us the slip in the past, and you can believe me when I say that his death will end organized rustling in this county.'

'But there were local men involved,' Hilt mused.

'That's right. We busted their outfit yesterday.' Clarke surveyed the vast extent of the canyon, and ordered two of his men to check out the cattle that could be seen grazing in the higher reaches. 'From what I've picked up about this local situation, I reckon Catlin and that posse are the only ones not accounted for. But we'll put that right soon as we get back to town. Thanks for your help, Smith. I reckon you'll be riding back to Diamond 0 now.'

'Yeah. I'm feeling a mite uneasy because Catlin is

out there somewhere and I got no idea which way he's planning to jump.'

'I don't reckon he'll hit Diamond O. That's been tried twice in the last two days and didn't work.'

'Only because I was there.' Hilt grimaced. 'I hope you're right, Captain.' He turned to his horse and swung into the saddle, then lifted a hand. 'So long.'

He rode to the arroyo, passed along it to the open range, then turned in the direction of the Ormond ranch. The buckskin was tired and he treated it gently, moving at a canter to conserve its strength.

The sun was high overhead when he sighted Diamond O. Some instinct had warned him against riding in openly and he slid out of his saddle beyond a rise. Taking his glasses, he left the buckskin grazing with trailing reins and sneaked forward to take a look at the distant ranch buildings.

At first the ranch looked deserted, and that impression filled him with foreboding. There was no movement anywhere. He focused his glasses and inspected the spread, his taut lips pulling even tighter when he saw two figures, apparently dead, sprawled in the dust of the yard to the left of the ranch house. He could not make out details and studied the buildings more intently.

He saw a guard with a rifle in his hands in the loft of the barn. The man was lounging on straw back from the doorway, but the imperceptibly moving oblong of sunlight bathing the interior had encompassed him. He was drowsing, and Hilt, studying his slack face, found himself looking at a stranger who had a deputy sheriff star glinting on his shirt front.

Hilt checked out the rest of the spread and discovered another deputy at one of the house windows overlooking the porch. He watched until he caught a glint of sunlight on the law badge the man was wearing. Checking the corral, he saw about twenty horses penned inside, half of them still saddled, and one of them was Catlin's big black stallion. Then he saw yet another guard at a bunkhouse window, covering the trampled dust of the big yard.

Easing back into total cover, Hilt pondered over what he had seen. That Catlin and the posse were here was obvious, but what were they doing? Those men forming the posse could not be townsmen on a lawful chore. They had to be some of Catlin's hardcases, and if the crooked sheriff was aware that his rustling partners had been beaten by the Rangers he would have pulled out of the county. But here he was, and apparently in control of the Diamond O.

Aware that there was nothing he could do until night came, Hilt settled down patiently and watched the ranch from cover, concerned by the lack of movement around the place. In normal circumstances there was always something happening on a ranch. So where were Art Weston and the Ormonds? He tried to keep his thoughts from turning on that subject and fought down impatience as time seemingly dragged by.

He stirred when, about the middle of the afternoon, a figure emerged from the house and walked leisurely across the yard to the corral. Using his glasses, Hilt watched the man's progress, and a thrill of anticipation touched him when the man

147

took a lariat from a saddle on the corral fence and tried to rope Catlin's black stallion. Hilt expected a tussle between man and bad-tempered horse.

In an instant all the horses in the corral were milling around nervously, and the black, when it realized it was the centre of the man's attention, whirled and dodged like a four-legged demon, easily avoiding the rope cast unerringly at it. After narrowly missing the black for the fourth time, the man coiled the rope and caught up another animal which was already saddled. Swinging into leather, he moved in determinedly on the black.

There followed a relentless fight between the man and the black, but the man knew what he was doing, and eventually caught the reins of the the big stallion and led it, rearing and trying to bite, to the gate in the corral. Hilt grinned in pure appreciation of the man's ability and watched his ride back to the porch leading the black.

Catlin emerged from the house and Hilt studied him through the glasses. The sheriff was completely at ease, stretching his arms as he looked around. Hilt ducked out of sight, aware that the slightest glint of sunlight on his field-glasses could warn the crooked lawman of his presence. He watched from cover as Catlin swung into his saddle and put the black through a process that was intended to make it amenable to riding.

The black bucked and craw-fished, doing everything but rolling on the ground, and Catlin stayed with it, fanning the air with his hat as he fought the spirited animal for mastery. The black bucked one last time, then ceased its resistance and became docile, but when it got close to the horse at the hitching rail by the porch it stretched its neck and sank its teeth into the animal's rump.

Catlin gave orders to the man on the porch and then turned the black and rode at a gallop for the open gateway, sending the black on at a furious pace. Away from the ranch, he followed the trail to town and soon disappeared beyond a rise.

Hilt pondered the significance of Catlin's departure but wasted no time. He went back to the buckskin, climbed into the saddle, and started a circuitous ride around the ranch, staying in cover until he reached the rear of the bunkhouse, mindful that hidden eyes were watching all approaches to the buildings.

Leaving the buckskin in deep cover in a draw, Hilt checked his pistol, then went forward on foot, angling for the bunkhouse to reach it at the end furthest from the house. The end of the building was windowless, and Hilt gained it without incident to stand against the hot boards, listening intently. He saw a long crack in one of the boards and applied his eyes to it, which enabled him to see the interior of the building. At first glance he saw a deputy standing by one of the front windows, but otherwise the bunkhouse appeared to be deserted. There was no sign of the Diamond O crew.

Hilt moved to the front corner of the building and took a one-eyed look around it to survey the yard. There was no movement anywhere, and, with a quick stride, he stepped around the corner and entered the bunkhouse by the nearby door. A board creaked under his foot and the deputy jerked into full wakefulness, turning to face him, lifting his rifle.

'You'll never make it,' Hilt warned, and the man froze, his muzzle still pointing upwards. 'Put it down gently on that bunk and step away from it, then put your hands up.'

The man paused for an interminable moment, considering his chances, then obeyed. He got rid of the rifle and raised his hands as he stepped into the centre of the bunkhouse.

'Where in hell did you come from?' he snarled. 'I never heard a blamed thing.'

'You were half asleep,' Hilt retorted. 'What's going on around here? Where's the Diamond O crew?'

'We caught 'em napping when we took over the place.'

Hilt regarded the man, who was tall and lean, with the look of a hardcase about him. He was bearded and dirty, wearing a gunbelt and two holstered pistols.

'Get rid of your gunbelt,' Hilt said, and waited until the man had obeyed. 'Now tell me what your orders are. What is Catlin doing here? Where are the Ormonds?'

'You got a lot of questions.' The man shrugged. 'If you want answers then go over to the house and talk to Catlin, because I don't know nothing. I was told to watch the yard and kill anyone I saw sneaking in.'

'Who is expected to come sneaking in?' Hilt demanded.

'You, I guess.' The man shrugged. 'And that's what you did, huh? And caught me cold. I heard tell there's a gunnie stepped in for the Ormonds who's been shooting the hell out of our bunch, and Catlin ain't taking any chances on you.'

'How many are there in the posse?' Hilt asked.

'More than you can handle, and a couple of them are watching the Ormonds to kill them if anyone tries to get in here. You're wasting your time, mister.'

Hilt went forward and grasped the man's shoulder, pushing him around. His gun barrel rose and fell in a swift arc, crashing against the man's right temple. Catching the man as he slumped, Hilt lowered him to the floor. He holstered his gun, took a lariat that was lying on a bunk, and trussed the man securely. The man regained his senses and looked up at Hilt with fury in his eyes.

'If I hear any noise coming out of you I'll be the first one back,' Hilt warned the man. 'And I'll gut-shoot you. Do you understand?'

The man nodded and Hilt picked up his rifle and went to the door. He was about to sneak out when he heard the sound of boots in the yard. Moving to a window, he peered out and saw a man coming from the house.

'Hey, Arlen, are you asleep in there?' the man called, as he came into the bunkhouse. He saw Hilt waiting with levelled pistol and immediately raised his hands, his jaw agape in shock.

'You've got some sense,' Hilt observed.

'Heck, I was in the Black Ace when you plugged Ben Hussey,' the man replied. 'I never saw a faster

151

draw than yours. You got me cold.'

'If you want to stay alive then do like I say,' Hilt replied. He disarmed the man and then said, 'I saw Catlin ride out: where's he gone and for how long?'

'He gone back to town. We had a rider in from Big D just after we got here. The Rangers caught Downey cold and killed most of the Big D outfit. Catlin needs to know what's happening now, if the Rangers went on to town.'

'How many men in the house?' Hilt asked.

'Near a dozen. They've turned the place into a fort. Even you couldn't get the drop on them.'

'Where are the Ormonds being held?'

'In the kitchen. The gal is cooking food. The old man and the son are hogtied. There's two men watching them.'

Hilt's mind was working fast, recalling what he knew of the layout of the house, and he decided that if he could free the Ormonds he could beat this set-up. He struck the man with the barrel of his pistol, then hogtied him while he was senseless.

Leaving the bunkhouse, he went around to the back and eased forward to the end nearest the house. Peering around the corner, he studied the cookshack, which was slightly to the left, back out of line between the bunkhouse and the ranch house. Acting on an impulse, he holstered his gun, pulled his Stetson low over his eyes, and stepped into the open to walk to the cookshack.

Reaching the shack, he pushed open the door and entered. It was empty, and he crossed to the window and studied the side of the ranch house. There was

152

a window in the end of the house that overlooked the yard and the area that Hilt wished to cross. His gaze went to the two bodies lying in the dust, and shock hit him hard when he saw that one of them was Art Weston, on his face and with blood on his shirt. Hilt gritted his teeth and suppressed a sigh. He went to the door and left the shack boldly, as if he had every right to be walking around.

He kept his right hand close to the butt of his holstered gun, and was faintly surprised when he reached the side of the house without incident. He went around to the back and made for the kitchen door, drawing his gun as he reached it.

Ducking below the kitchen window, he straightened beside the door, then eased back to the window and peered inside the big room. Sue Ormond and the housekeeper were cooking. Chuck Ormond was lounging in a big leather chair, his face showing shock and discomfort. There was fresh blood on the bandage around his chest and shoulder from having been moved down from his bedroom. Billy Ormond was bound to a kitchen chair, and there was a big bruise on the left side of the youngster's head where he had been pistol-whipped. Two possemen were in the room, both seated at the table. The inner kitchen door was closed, and Hilt hoped that the outer one, which he approached immediately, was not locked. He drew his gun and cocked it.

Grasping the handle gently, Hilt tried the door, and was relieved when it opened noiselessly. He thrust it wide and stepped into the kitchen, his big .45 levelled, his wrist jammed against his right hip.

The two men at the table froze in the act of spring-ing up and were cowed by the black muzzle of Hilt's deadly gun.

There was shocked silence in the kitchen. Both women froze at his entrance and remained gazing fixedly at him. Billy Ormond had jerked up as the door opened, and then began to grin. Chuck Ormond gazed at Hilt as if he were a ghost.

'Nobody move, and stay quiet,' Hilt ordered. He went to the two men in turn, relieving them of weapons. Both men sat with their hands in plain view of the table, scarcely breathing in their shock. Hilt glanced at Sue. 'Cut Billy free,' he suggested, and she picked up a carving knife and approached her brother.

Billy sprang to his feet when he was free and grabbed up the two guns the possemen had discarded. 'Am I glad to see you, Blaine,' he gasped. 'I knew you'd turn up. Now we can handle Catlin.'

'Tie those two and keep them quiet,' Hilt ordered.

'With pleasure.' Billy obeyed with alacrity. 'There are about ten of Catlin's men around. With these two, there are six in the house.'

'I'll take care of them.' Hilt moved to the inner door. 'Stay here, Billy, and protect your family.'

Hilt waited until the two possemen were bound, then opened the door and peered out into the passage. It was gloomy in the house. He slipped out of the kitchen and went toward the front of the house, remembering the guard he had seen at one of the windows overlooking the porch.

There were two men in the big room at the front

of the house, both gazing moodily out at the yard. Hilt slid around the half opened door and placed his back against the rear wall beside it. When he thumbed back the hammer of his gun the three clicks sounded monstrously loud in the heavy silence. Both possemen started in shock, then came swinging round to face him. One was holding a rifle, and lifted it quickly. The other moved his right hand to his holstered pistol.

Hilt squeezed his trigger. The crash of the detonation shook the room, chasing out the brooding silence. His bullet took the nearest man in the centre of the chest. The man folded instantly, every joint in his body relaxing as the slug tore through his heart. Hilt swung his gun. The second man was trying desperately to bring his rifle into line, and fired before he could draw a bead on Hilt. The bullet smashed one of the big front windows. Hilt shot the man through the heart.

Turning instantly, Hilt moved into the doorway and covered the passage leading to the rear of the house. There were doors opening off it on either side and he watched them intently. The stairs were to his left. He waited while gun echoes faded, poised for action. Boots thumped overhead, and then a voice called from above, demanding to know what had happened.

'Come down and find out,' Hilt replied.

A door opened noisily along the passage and a man peered out. Hilt fired a shot that splintered woodwork and the man ducked back out of sight. The next instant a hand holding a gun came into

view and triggered off several shots that flew harmlessly along the passage. Hilt dropped to one knee
and waited. The man's head appeared in the doorway and Hilt snapped a shot at it. The bullet struck
home. Blood flew and the man staggered out of the
doorway, fell to his knees and slumped to the floor.

Two men appeared together from a doorway
further back on the right. Both triggered ready
Colts, aiming about chest high on a standing man,
and Hilt heard slugs crackle over his head. He
returned fire, boring one man through the chest and
sending a bullet through the head of the second.
Then he waited while an uneasy silence returned,
feeding fresh cartridges into his empty cylinder.

Boots sounded upstairs and he closed his pistol
and canted the muzzle slightly. He heard glass
splintering in one of the bedrooms, and then a
thump outside as someone jumped out of an upper
window and landed on the ground. He went to a
window, peered out, and saw a man hobbling
towards the corral.

Hilt smashed the window with his gun barrel.
The sound of it attracted the man, who whirled and
lifted his gun, firing quickly. As Hilt returned fire, a
bullet struck his left upper arm. Outside, the man
went down. Hilt clenched his teeth against the pain
that flared in his arm. Then he heard the sound of a
horse coming fast into the yard.

Alarm filled him. He cocked his gun and moved to
the nearest front window. A rider was approaching
the porch, and Hilt forced a grin. It was Catlin,
astride his big black stallion. Hilt went to the door,

gun ready. He waited until Catlin reached the porch, then stepped outside, covering the man. Catlin reined in and sat motionless, his bronzed face expressionless. Then he shook his head and grinned ruefully.

'I was on my way to town when I heard the shooting back here,' he said, 'and I reckoned it was you. Have you killed off my men?'

'Just about.' Hilt clenched his teeth against the pain spreading through his arm. 'Now it's your turn.'

'You gonna kill me in cold blood?'

'Why not? You're a snake.'

'You don't reckon you can take me from an even break, huh?' Catlin laughed harshly.

Anger welled up in Hilt's mind. Catlin reached for his gun in a fast draw. Hilt was struggling against the shock of his wound. He saw Catlin's gun appear and set his own hand into motion.

The two pistols exploded simultaneously. Hilt felt the numbing strike of a bullet in his right thigh and fell backwards against the wall. Catlin pitched sideways out of his saddle, blood on his forehead marking the strike of Hilt's bullet.

Hilt lowered his gun and fell into the rocker on the porch, retaining his hold on his pistol. There was movement at his side and he looked up quickly to see Billy coming to him. He heard the pounding of many horses approaching and started up, raising his gun. A dozen riders were coming across the yard and he steeled himself to face them. But Billy reached out and pushed down his lethal gun.

'You don't need it,' the youngster said joyfully.

157

'Them's Rangers. It's all over, Blaine. You've beaten Catlin.'

Hilt smiled and let his mind run over the events that had occurred since his arrival. He nodded and holstered his gun, then gripped his injured left arm with his deadly right hand. Blood was dripping copiously and the pain was shocking. But relief filled him. It was all over! With Catlin's death he was free of his self-imposed obligation to fight for the Diamond O, and when his wounds had healed he could get back to what he was doing before he came to Diamond O – hunting Buck Dunne.

There was movement at his side and he looked round at Sue as she emerged from the house. Shock came to her face when she saw that he was hurt, and her gentle fingers immediately grasped his arm, ready to help. He smiled. Everything was fine . . .